Homebody Unit 362 was a good place to get out of – except that there wasn't anywhere else to go. Outside the Ecoshield, which sealed it into an invisible capsule, lay a wasteland of poisoned air, barren soil, grotesque plant and animal mutations. And inside there were only other, identical Homebody Units, each with its Bevvie Lounge, its DormSpaces, its Viddy to plug into for programmes you could see, hear, taste, touch and smell – which provided everything, in fact, except *responsibility* for your experience.

And responsibility was what Dano craved. He hated his aimless life as a Hopeful, with a catalogueful of sportsgear, nothing to look forward to but one day becoming a Primer, with a zoomdrive car and a rabbit-hutch home – and, eventually, a Senior Citizen with nothing at all. Dano felt the twenty-first century was the wrong time for him to be around in. But, until he learnt Uncle Lipton's secret, he didn't see what he could do about it.

Uncle Lipton was a hundred and thirty-seven years old. He had been dosed with Xtend, a special life-prolonging drug developed for astronauts setting off on very long voyages back in the twentieth century. But the spaceshot in which he took part proved disastrous and he returned to Earth a failure, a man you turned the cameras away from. But he still had a supply of Xtend. And he was to discover that the drug had a second, even stranger power ...

Time Trap is the story of the secret Uncle Lipton shared with Dano – fantastically rewarding to begin with, cruelly disappointing later on – and, like all Nicholas Fisk's books, it is a compulsive read. Clever, puzzling, sad and grimly funny by turn, this glimpse into the future will keep you on tenterhooks till the last page.

Other Nicholas Fisk titles in Puffins are:

Grinny
Space Hostages
Trillions

Nicholas Fisk
Time Trap

Puffin Books
in association with Victor Gollancz
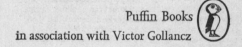

Puffin Books, Penguin Books Ltd, Harmondsworth
Middlesex, England
Penguin Books, 625 Madison Avenue,
New York, New York 10022, U.S.A.
Penguin Books Australia Ltd, Ringwood,
Victoria, Australia
Penguin Books Canada Ltd, 2801 John Street,
Markham, Ontario, Canada L3R 1B4
Penguin Books (N.Z.) Ltd, 182–190 Wairau Road,
Auckland 10, New Zealand

First published by Victor Gollancz 1976
Published in Puffin Books 1979

Copyright © Nicholas Fisk, 1976
All rights reserved

Made and printed in Great Britain by
Hazell Watson & Viney Ltd, Aylesbury, Bucks
Set in Linotype Juliana

Do you know what circular insanity is? It's the sort of insanity that takes you full circle to the point from which you started.

For example – do you know a song that goes *There's a hole in my bucket, Eliza, Eliza?* I bet you don't. A century and more before your time, that song. This is 2079. When was *Eliza* last sung, I wonder? 1970, 1980, 2001? Never mind – the song shows just what is meant by circular insanity. It's a joke duet sung by a stupid boy and a girl to a sad, silly, whining tune. The boy holds a bucket with a hole in it. He sings –

> There's a hole in my bucket, Eliza, Eliza,
> There's a hole in my bucket, Eliza, a hole.
> With what shall I mend it, Eliza, Eliza,
> With what shall I mend it, Eliza, with what?

She replies. She tells the boy to mend the bucket with straw.

He says, with what shall I cut it?
She says, with a knife.
The knife is blunt. With what shall I sharpen it, he asks.
She says, with a stone.
He says, with what shall I wet the stone?
She says, with water.
He says, in what shall I fetch it, Eliza, Eliza?
She says, in a bucket.
And he says – ah, you've guessed it – he says,

> But there's a hole in my bucket, Eliza, Eliza!

That's circular insanity. And circular insanity is what I'm suffering from.

Circular insanity and my Galactic Uncle Lipton.

He's not really my uncle, of course. I began calling him uncle years ago, when I was young and his magic was still real and alive to me. Now it's a habit.

There he is, over there with the other Oldies. You're seeing him at his worst. Just look at him! It's his tot time, his 'Cheers, chaps!' time. He's beginning to nudge and wink and hunch his shoulders. He's reaching into his back pocket. Now it's out, the leather-bound antique silver flask, almost hidden in his big paw. Nudge, wink, chortle. Some of the other old phonies are looking embarrassed – look, one's walking away! – but Galactic Uncle Lipton takes no notice, he tips the silver flask over the Bevvie mug. Glig-glog-glug. Chortle wink nudge. Aaaaah! Smack-smack! Uncle Lipton has had his little tot! Uncle Lipton has defied the NO ALCOHOL notices on the wall! The daring of him! The defiance of authority! The reckless courage of the man! Uncle Lipton is a deuced fine chap!

But not really, of course. What I know and he knows and the others don't know is that Uncle Lipton has Official Authority to drink himself rotten. The Official Authority *wants* him to drink himself into a seizure – would go down on its hands and knees to *beg* him to kill himself with the stuff.

Now is your cue to look me straight in the eye and say 'Very well. They want him to die. And how about you, Dano Gazzard? Do *you* want him to die?' And I'm supposed to flinch and look uneasy, before answering 'Of course not!' What else can I answer? I'm as much a part of Uncle Lipton as his silver flask (ask him to show you the hallmark, he'll like that). I'm tied to Uncle. He's got me in his pocket, just like that flask. And I'll never get out of it as long as Uncle Lipton lives. Because if he goes, I'd go. If I want to live, I have to want Uncle Lipton to live. I have to help him to keep alive, actually help him . . .

There's another reason. Although I sound bitter about Uncle Lipton – although I make him sound just a fat old relic – there's still that magic I mentioned. The magic began in my childhood, in the days when there was only one person in the world who could tell me stories and truths that made me hold my breath. He picked on me because, as he used to tell me, 'You've got imagination, boy. You're different.' I picked on him for just the same reason. I can see myself now, sitting at his feet, wide-eyed and boggling, while he transported me light-years away from 2079 and the Homebody Unit. I can see him, too – not booming and shouting, not the Uncle Lipton of the Bevvie Lounge – just a big, quiet, deep-voiced, rumbling figure who might at any moment dig up yet another treasure from his limitless store.

'But why did your bicycle have three speeds, Uncle?' 'Ah, that was because –' and he'd tell me, and I'd imagine myself riding through a forest (a forest! Thousands of real trees, big trees!) on a green bicycle, pedalling mile after mile ...

'But when you were in space, drinking liquids, what happened if you spilled a drop? What did the spilled stuff *do*?' 'Ah, well, that could be amusing. You see –' and he'd tell me, and I'd see myself as an astronaut, an adventurer at the controls of a metal township hurtling through nothingness on its way to an incredible destination.

Nobody else in the Homebody Unit wanted to know these things. I did. Nobody – except a few Topmosts of the Official Authority – knew Uncle Lipton's secret. I alone did – and you must admit, it's an amazing secret. The fact is (and it is a fact, not just another of Uncle Lipton's Bevvie Lounge stories) that he might live for another hundred years ... *and has already lived one hundred and thirty-seven years!*

As I say, no one here in Homebody Unit 362 knows that. But then, nobody in Unit 362 knows anything very much. They just amble about doing their thing. A pretty dull thing it is. The old ones drink True T and Coffymost and all the other synths in the Bevvie Lounge. Some of them drink gallons a day, I swear they do. Sometimes, when they get their Senior Citizen Credits and it's a Saturday night – they can drink alcohol then – they lash out and buy each other Wizzky or Brand-E or =Gin. Some of them even pretend to get drunk on the stuff though it isn't strong enough to wiffle a mouse. None of them has even tasted the real thing, of course (but I have. In the 1940s).

Then we've got the Primers, the middle-aged ones. Primers because they're supposed to be in the prime of life. I can only just bring myself to write about them. Even the ones with jobs or the ones with filled Kiddie Quotas (the full quota is two children, precisely two; when I was an evacuee in the 1940s, one of the kids I was with came from a family of *nine* children) – even the Primers with something to do, something real in their lives, are just Permitted Proudies. The Official Authority permits them to be proud of their zoomdrive cars, proud of their horrible homes (I'd call them hutches), proud of their ten-foot-square back gardens (look! a real shrub!) – yes and proud of their Partners, their wives. Proud even of them! They *like* being Proudies.

But I've got pride too and I will not, repeat will not, write about the Partners. I suppose there was some dignity for women in the days when they had jobs or became wives – when they actually had to *do* something, bring up children, cook and worry and be nice when they didn't feel like it. But this is 2079 and the State brings up the children. They hardly see their parents until they are Teens. So the Primers haven't anything to do, and the Partners . . .

Look, I could tell you everything you need to know about the typical Partner in Unit 362 or any other Unit simply by showing you the only thing she ever reads, the Catalogue. You press the buttons and up comes the Catalogue on the Viddy wall – endless beauty aids, endless things to make you thin here, sticking out there, firm or soft or pneumatic or bunjy in the other place . . . endless paints and wigs and stilts and uplifts and soothers and smoothers. The Catalogue is the only thing they ever read, I really mean it.

Then there's us. Oh, you'd just love us. The Hopefuls, they call us, the Teens. First I was a Bud, then a Blossom or Kiddie, and now I'm a Hopeful, a Teen. Just like the others, I've got a skimmer that can do 100 mph before you even hit the plus-drive booster. I've got all the sportsgear in the Catalogue. I've even got some muscles left over from that brief period when I lived in the 1940s, one hundred and thirty-something years ago, when I was twelve.

But back to the present. In the last two years, I've experienced all the official stuff – the Grand Adventure (twice), Onward!, Your Awakening Body, the lot. Just like all the others, I might actually *do* something one day, not just sit facing the Viddy wall. I've already killed three people with my skimmer, but that hardly counts – they were all Senior Citizens. I mean really *do something*, something real, something you can't talk yourself out of if it goes wrong (Teen skimmer accidents, for instance, are officially O.K., like beatings up).

No, I want something with meaning. Something like the 1940s, the only time I really lived and *did* things.

But of course I couldn't have done those things without Uncle Lipton. I can't really do anything without Uncle Lipton. He's got me in his pocket all right.

I've just been writing on and on, I apologize. I suppose it doesn't make much sense to you yet. But I like writing for its own sake, it gets you near *doing* something, something of your own. And I'm proud of my secret vice, my writing. Not many people can write at all – what would be the point these days, with the Viddy doing everything for you? – so just sitting down and writing makes me feel important. And reading Uncle Lipton's books has given me a taste for written words. He has all these books, hundreds of them. I don't think he reads them any more. He just talks about them. But to me, the books really mean something.

Just now, I wrote that the Viddy does everything for you. I should rewrite that. It does everything and nothing. You don't really experience anything when you hook yourself up to the Viddy, do you? Sight, sound, touch, taste, smell – they're all there, I admit it. The Viddy really does provide it all. All but for one thing – *responsibility*. It's because you have no *responsibility* for the things happening on the Viddy that you can make no real *response*. People come up to you and you say 'Wow! Fantass! Peakview! That programme last night when the big skimmers were blasting that town apart! – and the scene in the starship with the pressure leak! – I thought I'd *die*!'

But that's the whole point, you *didn't* think you would die. You thought that when the programme was over, you'd go to bed and that's what you did. So you couldn't really respond, could you? Because you weren't responsible, were you?

If you'd been in England during the 1940s you really would have responded. There were bombs – only little ones, not fission bombs – but they were real and they were falling on you and *you couldn't switch them off*. Do you see the difference?

Now, where was I? I remember, I was going to start explaining what I am writing about. Here we go, then.

Once, my Uncle Lipton was a really important man. He was important because he was going to the Galaxy. He was one of the international crew of the spaceship, the biggest and best spaceship the world had ever known.

The date was 1983. Get that in your mind – 1983 – or you'll never follow me.

In 1983, Uncle Lipton was exactly forty-one years old. So he was born in 1942.

In 1942, what was known as World War II was being

fought. It was a very big war – as big as the war of 2029 and longer-lasting. Russia, America and the British Empire were fighting Germany, Italy and other European countries and also Japan. The war ended in 1945, when Uncle Lipton was still a little child.

Uncle Lipton grew up where he was born, in Euroseven. They called it England then, of course. As he grew, he played war games like all the other children. He could just remember things about World War II – the aeroplanes in the sky, for instance – and he grew up thinking that the war must have been a very wonderful time.

When he was old enough he took up flying, first with the Royal Air Force, then in civil aviation (they had big airliners even in those days) and then, in his thirties, with the RAF again. Space travel was just beginning. Uncle Lipton was fascinated by space travel. Through his RAF training, he became the sort of person needed to man a spaceship. He was selected for the shot that was going to take man to the Galaxy in 1983.

We didn't set foot in any part of the Galaxy until 2004, you say? Quite right, we didn't. Uncle Lipton took part in a complete disaster. Nearly complete, anyhow. The spaceshot petered out, most of the people in the ship died, somehow or other they got the messed-up ship back on this planet. Uncle Lipton survived and so did another dozen or so men and women. It might have been better if they had died. It would certainly have been better for me. If Uncle Lipton had died, I might be a contented little Hopeful or Teen or moron, instead of what I am. Which is, fed up.

But that is beside the point. Let's get on with the explaining. Uncle Lipton didn't get back to the Galaxy, but he did get back to Earth. He set out for the Galaxy amid all the fuss and hoo-hah and Viddy coverage that the very first Russian and American moonshots got, back in the 1960s and 70s. Big hero.

He came back a failure, a survivor, a man you turned the

cameras away from. Nobody wanted to remember the disastrous failure of the spaceshot. And no one wanted to think about the survivors, men like Uncle Lipton.

Nobody, that is, except a very few officials and scientists. To the scientists, he continued to be of interest, the greatest possible interest. Uncle Lipton, you see, had been given a drug called Xtend.

It makes me feel quite brave just writing that word down, really it does. To show how brave I am, I'll do it again. Xtend! And again. Xtend! If any official gets hold of this, his hair will turn white on the spot. Xtend Xtend Xtend!

Uncle Lipton's hair didn't turn white. That was the whole point of Xtend. You see, the spaceshot to the Galaxy was intended to take the crew and passengers millions and millions of miles. The people in the craft were in for a voyage that would last years – so many years that some of the people would very probably die on the voyage.

Uncle Lipton, as a member of the crew, could not be allowed to die. He was truly important. Therefore he and other key men and women were given the drug Xtend – the drug that extends human life. Xtend makes you live longer. Simple. Simply disastrous, as it turned out, because the shot missed – the survivors were brought back – and among them was Uncle Lipton, failed hero and confirmed pill-taker, whose life expectation (thanks to Xtend) was perhaps another two hundred years!

Just picture it. Here they come, the Galaxy failures, being carried off the spacecraft. They've been in space for about fifteen years. They've had an awful time. Some of the stretcher cases look incredibly old – white hair, skin falling away from their bones, mad eyes. Really, of course, no one on the ship is much above fifty-five, but some of them look ninety after what they've been through. All are dead or dying but one.

Ah, and here he comes: Uncle Lipton. He looks tired, perhaps. A trifle peaky. A little out of sorts. More than a little worried about the nasty silence, the absence of Viddy cameras, the non-heroes' non-welcome. But young, remarkably young! Hardly a day older! That Xtend stuff really did work, it really did keep the wrinkles at bay.

And ah, my friends, it did more than that. Xtend had unforeseen side effects. It not only kept the body young, it also stretched the mind. You'd better believe what it did to the mind! Uncle Lipton told me all about it. 'Listen!' he boomed. 'I'm going to astonish you! Tell you something you don't know!' He always likes to begin with words in exclamation marks – a sentence or two to tell you what a big wheel he is. Something dramatic.

'Something you don't know!' he continued. 'Something that only I know! Something I know here, here, *here*!' (tapping himself twice on the head and once on the heart). 'Something astounding ... ! ! !'

He told me all about what Xtend did to him, on the Galaxy flight. At first, the pills made him feel very lively and well. Then he started feeling too lively, particularly at night. He couldn't sleep, his mind wouldn't go to sleep. As the months went by, this led to depression and worry – he got so worried by his insomnia that it kept him awake at night, ha ha.

At last, Uncle Lipton told me, he found the answer to his insomnia. A staggering answer! An astonishing answer ! ! An answer that was like a blinding light in the darkness of a shuttered room ! ! ! etc. etc. In other words, exactly the answer that you or I would have found: instead of lying awake and thinking about things that made him miserable, he lay awake and thought about things that pleased him. He thought about the simply stupendous girls he had known (nudge nudge). He thought about good times with the boys (joke joke). And he thought about the past.

As I've already told you, the past had two meanings for Uncle Lipton, just as it has for all of us. There was his own past, which, up to the time I'm writing about, when Uncle

Lipton was on his way to the Galaxy, must have been success-ful and exciting. And there was his imagined past, the fan-tasy past centred on World War II. It's easy enough to work out which past he'd prefer to think about during those long sleepless nights. As a real-life young man he had become a pilot – but not a fighter pilot, not a POW! BAM! war pilot. His real-life piloting was second best to the dream piloting.

And although he had been one of the princely crew selec-ted to fly to the Galaxy – although he was about to become a hero, or so he thought – the Galaxy flight had become a bore, dragging on year after year. A bore ending in a failure.

So his night imaginings were all about World War II, the war he missed, the war that happened when he was a small boy. That was the past he really liked – the one he'd never had. If you think this is all theory, you should just hear Uncle Lipton talk. 'Bang on!' he booms. 'Wizard! Good show! Smashing!' All the words the World War II pilots used. All the words left over from a war he never experienced. Even today, more than a hundred and thirty years after that war, he still uses those words.

So there he is in the spaceship, up to the eyeballs in Xtend, tossing and turning on his bed and telling himself stories about World War II. In his imagination he's the pilot of a Spitfire, zooming down on a Messerschmidt 109. '*M-yeeaaaah!* Oh, damn poor show, wrong deflection! Flick roll, under his tail again, full boost, got him in the sights now! – *rat-tat-tat-tat-tat!* Bang on! Gosh, the hun's had it! Black smoke, bits flying off – smashing! Spiralling down now, better follow him down, he's going to prang ... WHOOMPH!' Later, back at base, a few words with the interrogating officer. 'Yes, well, actually sir, it *was* rather definite. Ginger here will confirm it. Me 109 as a matter of fact, sir. Yes sir, right down to the ground, went for a com-plete burton. About three miles inland. They should find his pranged kite all right, or what's left of it. Oh, thank you, sir, but I was just lucky, sir, just lucky ...' And so on and so on.

One of these sleepless nights, something strange happened to Uncle Lipton.

'I'll tell you something, boy,' he said. 'Something that will *astound* you! There I was, lying in the old pit in the spaceship trying to get a bit of shut-eye ... and thinking of the old days in the war, d'you see ... thinking about it pretty hard, the Spitfires and Hurricanes and all that – a Spit doing a victory roll, no sight like it! – when suddenly, boy, *there I was!* – there I was, I tell you, holding my mother's hand, walking along the high street. Toddling, rather. I was actually *there*, boy, actually there in the high street –'

'You mean, you remembered your childhood?' I said.

'No, no, *no*. I was *there*. She was pushing my pram, it had small wheels with white rubber tyres and shiny chromium-plated mudguards going rusty. She'd put the shopping bag in the pram and so I had to walk. The pram was full, d'you see. I was very tired, I was too young to walk properly and my mother was cross, she kept tugging at me and saying, "Come on, come *on*."'

'But that's just a memory, a vivid memory.'

'Wait a minute, I haven't finished yet. I've told you about ration books?'

He had. Ration books were paper books with coupons in them. You gave the shopkeeper some of the coupons and he gave you your ration of food. Ration books made sure you couldn't get more food than anyone else. Not only food – clothes, petrol, lots of things. Just the opposite of today, when the Official Authority twists your arm to make you buy more of everything that's Officially Authorized.

'The ration books,' Uncle Lipton went on, 'were absolutely priceless. If you lost your ration books, you'd had it. Couldn't buy food, had to queue up endlessly to get replacement books, very nasty business. Even a toddler knew about ration books – knew they were very important, mustn't be lost. I knew it. Anyhow, as we were walking along, the pram joggled over a bump and the ration books slipped out of my mother's handbag and fell on the pavement. I saw them fall, she didn't. Clear so far?'

'Yes,' I said patiently, 'quite clear.'

'I saved those ration books!' he said. 'I tugged at my mother's skirt and said, "Look, Mummy!" She stopped and picked up the books and kissed me and so on. When we got home, she was almost crying she was so relieved. She kept telling me what a good boy I was. She said she would give me a special treat for being so good. Do you know what she gave me?'

'No,' I said.

'Bread and butter with sugar on it!' shouted Uncle Lipton. 'That's what she gave me! Bread and butter and sugar! And I don't mind telling you, boy, it was the finest feast I've ever had in my life. I can taste it now, boy, taste it to this day!'

'Yes,' I said.

'Ah, but wait a minute!' said Uncle Lipton. 'You haven't heard the half of it yet. Forty years or so later, there came the time when I was lying in the spaceship, trying to get to sleep, thinking of those old days. And as I told you, I thought I was remembering that day again, trotting along with my mother. But somehow I knew that this time, I wasn't remembering – I was *living* it! It wasn't just *glimpses* of the past – it *was* the past! I tell you, boy, I looked at that pram with new eyes. I saw every little spot of rust on the mudguards. I saw where the shiny stuff on the hood had worn through at one corner and the fabric was splitting. I saw that the heels of my mother's shoes were worn down. I looked at my own legs and saw the little golden hairs on them. I was seeing it all for the first time, seeing it *real*. Living it!'

'Fantass,' I said, unenthusiastically.

'Then,' he continued, 'it happened. The ration books fell out, just as they had done before in my memories. They fell on the pavement, just the same. I paused. I hesitated. I started to bend down to pick them up . . .'

'Yes?' I said; I was interested now.

'Then I thought to myself, "No! I won't She's making me walk and walk and walk and I'm tired! I'll leave them where they are, leave them lying on the pavement, just to spite her!" And believe it or not, boy, that is precisely what I did. I left them there. Just left them lying there!'

'What happened then?' I asked.

'I fell into a dreamless sleep,' said Uncle Lipton, nodding solemnly.

'Oh,' I said.

'And in the morning, boy, I reached out my hand and grasped the little plastic bottle containing the Xtend tablets. I put a tablet in the palm of my hand and looked at it, long and hard ...' He put an imaginary tablet in his hand and looked at it long and hard. 'Then – I took one gulp and swallowed time! See what I mean, laddie? See what I mean?'

'Fantass,' I said, bored again. 'I must be going now, Uncle Lipton.'

I didn't see what he meant and, to use his own phrase, I couldn't have cared less.

Yet what he told me was one of the most important things the world has ever known.

Uncle Lipton told me all this a year ago. I must have walked around for a week or more with the key to the past (and perhaps the future) still rattling about in my deaf ears and stupid brain. But I never heard, never thought.

The penny didn't drop (that's another phrase Uncle Lipton uses – a penny was a coin used before world cash credits came in), the penny didn't drop until one day, when I was in a hurry, I saw Uncle Lipton and shouted, 'What's the time, Uncle Lipton?' He wears a wristwatch, a fantastic thing, you have to wind its clockwork each night. He looked at this ridiculous relic and said, '*Any time you like, boy!*'

He didn't boom out these words, he said them quietly and sneakily as if he didn't want them overheard.

This quietness was so unlike him that it stopped me dead.

As I stopped, I thought. As I thought, the whole thing hit me like an out-of-control skimmer. I went over to him and said, 'What?'

'You can close your mouth if you've finished speaking, laddie,' he said. I must have been gaping at him. Then he repeated, 'Any time you like. Any time at all. The past is best for beginners.'

I said, 'What?' again, or something equally brilliant, and he took my arm and pulled me away from the crowd. Finding somewhere to be alone is quite a problem in Homebody Unit 362, but he managed.

He said, 'Look, lad, how would you like a real adventure? Away from all this?'

I said, 'What?' once again and he went on.

'It's not so easy any more,' he said. 'I get a little frightened of doing it alone. I admit it; windy. I've blotted my copybook once or twice and someone might remember. A chance meeting ... they weren't fools then, you know, not fools at all. I want to go back, yet I'm afraid to go back. I might make mistakes again, it's so easy to make the mistake –'

'I don't understand!' I said. And I didn't understand most of it. But I did understand the most important part.

I understood that when Uncle Lipton told me about being a little boy again, and the pram and the ration books and everything, he was telling me the truth. He really had gone back in time, it wasn't just his imagination.

I understood why he had said, 'Any time you like!' in that funny way.

I understood that Xtend could not only stop his body's decay through time: it could also free his body to move in time.

'You understand all right, boy!' he said urgently. 'We can go back! Go back together! Take a holiday in those old days, the *real* days ... You'd like it, boy, really you would, I promise you would!' He was almost pleading with me.

'But why take me?' I said. 'Why take anyone?'

'I just told you,' he said. 'It's lonely. People get to *sense* something about you. The more they get to know you the more they sense that you're different. And then there are the tablets. Xtend. I haven't got unlimited stocks left, you know. Xtend is now in short supply. Definitely. And I seem to need more and more of the stuff to get results. Bigger dose each time. Now, you wouldn't need such a big dose, and we might trigger each other off it we *both* took the stuff. Get me?'

'You mean twice the power ... with only one and a half times the number of Xtends?' I said. 'But you'd still be using more Xtends.'

'But it might work out that you could learn to take us *both* back,' he said, all excited. 'And on a smaller Xtend ration. Get it?'

'I suppose so,' I said doubtfully. Then – remembering how badly I wanted to make the trip – I said, 'Yes. Definitely!'

'And then there's yet *another* thing,' said Uncle Lipton, looking very solemn. 'There's always the risk of making the mistake again.'

'What mistake?'

'Of changing something. Look, I'll be frank with you, son. You know I like a drink and all that, just a drink to keep me going, you know what I mean.'

I said, 'Yes.' I knew what he meant all right.

'Well, the drink then was different, they made it differently. The real stuff, nearly all alcohol. Well, I had too much to drink once on one of my trips – it was in 1939, a year or two before I was born, I'd gone back to the beginning of the war – I had a drink too many, and I hit a man. He fell over and gave his head one hell of a bang, a really nasty knock. They put him in hospital. His skull was fractured. They didn't know how to deal with things like that in those days and the man got worse, he became a sort of loonie – you know, out of his mind. Well, you see, I did that!'

'So what? People get hit all the time. The skimmers, they're always hitting people –'

'Don't be stupid, lad, try not to be stupid! That's different, not the same thing at all. That's *now*, when things are still happening. But you can't go back to *then* and change things that have already happened! Use your loaf, laddie, use your loaf!'

I used my loaf and understood. Suppose, for instance, you went back in time and shot Hitler, or poisoned Churchill, or murdered Stalin (they were topmost, peakview national leaders of World War II). If you did that, you'd change history, wouldn't you? But history has already happened. It cannot and must not change.

Let me give you another instance. Suppose you went back in time and somehow got rid of the men who developed the first atom bomb that was dropped on the Japanese: how much longer would the war have lasted? Would the same side still have won? Would there be, today, a Unit 362? Would I be alive? Would you? Would we be living the same sort of life?

Once history has happened, can it be un-happened? And if you did un-happen it, what would happen to us – here – now?

Suppose, even, that you did what Uncle Lipton did – changed a single, unimportant man's life. What else have you changed? What about his wife, his sons, his grandsons?

'That's *the* mistake?' I said.

'*The* mistake,' said Uncle Lipton. 'The small things – I don't mind taking a risk with them. Once, in 1941, I stole a chicken. Killed and ate it. Well, I haven't got a guilty conscience about that, just one chicken can't make any difference to history.' He looked at me, worriedly, and said, 'It can't, can it?'

'No, I don't think so. No, of course not. But,' I asked, 'what will they say when we've gone?' By 'they', I meant the Official Authority.

'I hadn't thought of that,' he said. 'They might make a fuss if you disappeared. It's all right for me, of course, I'm a special case. A very special case, lad. They just threaten me, but they've never done anything yet.'

'You mean, they hope you won't come back,' I said cheekily.

He gave me a fishy look and said, 'You could put it that way. They'd like to see the back of me, boy. Like to see your Uncle Lipton dead. Dead scared of Uncle Lipton and what he represents. The olden days, lad, the olden ways! Ha!'

He thought about this for a moment or two and then said, 'But I'm half dead already, boy! So are you in this dead-and-alive hole!'

When he said this, I knew I would do whatever he suggested. Half dead. That's just what I am, just what you are. Half dead!

Just in case my writings ever become Major Historical Discoveries, I'll describe a Homebody Unit of 2079 – and at the same time explain why most of us are half dead with boredom.

Here we are in Homebody 362. Not very big, is it? Small, in fact. Poky, even. A good place to get out of.

But there isn't a way out. The Ecoshield seals the whole colony of Homebody Units inside an invisible capsule. Admittedly you can pass through the Ecoshield, just as a needle can pass through a soap bubble : but I wouldn't if I were you. For on the other side, there could be anything. Poisonous air, deadly dust, plants and berries that can grow only by torturing themselves into shapes they were never meant to have, wild flowers that writhe their stems into knots and choke before they mature, crazed insects that eat themselves, two-headed rodents with blind milky eyes, petrified trees that ring like metal when you strike them, barren soil covered by a crust of what looks like molten glass . . .

No, you're better off inside.

This is my bed. There are exactly 50 centimetres between my bed and those next to it. The cupboard containing my whole personal life, including this writing, is two metres high and 45 centimetres wide. The 35-centimetre space between the top of my cupboard and the ceiling MUST BE KEPT CLEAR – see the notice.

There are eleven other people in my DormSpace (DS 362/H – the H stands for Hopefuls). So we are all Hopefuls of one sex or another (or neither). We all look alike when we are dressed except that our bodies fill out our Official Authority clothes differently. Most of us think alike.

You've had enough of DS 362/H? Follow me, I'll show you the rest. It won't take long, how could it?

That biggish building is the Bevvie Lounge and the people clambering about on its roof are two lucky Hopefuls who've been allotted the privilege of some Work Hours. They are tightening up the tower on top of the Bevvie building. The tower is four metres high, no less! – and thus sticks out from the other buildings. All Bevvie Lounges have towers made from unikits and we are encouraged to make our tower different from other Homebody Units' towers. Ours is different because it is painted green and red. It is still more different because it is falling over to one side; somebody inside the Bevvie Lounge must have sneezed.

Putting the tower right will take the workers the rest of the day. They will do the job all wrong so as to give others the chance to put in some Work Hours. There are never enough Work Hours to go round.

There's the skimmer pile. The skimmers are designed to be stacked up on top of each other. That's my skimmer, third from the top. Those five people staring at the skimmers are Permitted Proudies. All five are checking the skimmers; all five have lists and each list is the same. As I said, there are never enough Work Hours to go round.

They give skimmers to us Hopefuls so we can give ourselves a thrill now and then, even hurt someone seriously (big thrill, that). But the rest of the time we just do what the Official Authority wants us to do. And when we've done that we plug into the Viddy, the Viddy, the Viddy, the Viddy, the Viddy . . .

(Has it ever occurred to you that we are not real at all – but the Viddy is? Put it another way : do we watch the Viddy, or is Viddy watching us? Have you ever thought that you yourself might be just part of the Viddy's programme – a component it can't do without?)

Dorm, Bevvie Lounge, skimmers, Viddy . . . Is there any more I can tell you about Homebody Unit 362 and 2079? I don't think so, not just now. I can't stand the excitement of writing about them and you're yawning too.

And here was Uncle Lipton offering me the chance to get away, to escape, to be not just half alive but all alive ! To take a real risk, meet a real danger ! I said : 'Uncle Lipton, we've got to go and I don't care what the Official Authority says. Besides, they'd never punish me –'

He said, 'Steady, boy. I know they won't punish you – not in the sense of giving you a good smacked bottom, like in the old days – but they could neutralize you. I don't think they would, but they could.'

'I don't care,' I said. I didn't. I'm neutralized enough already. What worse can they do? Stop me connecting? But I don't want to connect. I've had enough Viddy for the rest of my life. I've got my writing and that's like a picture show running in my head whenever I want it.

They might trank me? I've never seen that as a punishment. I admit the tranks look a bit weird stumbling around and blundering into things, but who's the sufferer – the person who turns his head away and looks embarrassed, or the trank himself? I don't mind an unlimited spell of tranquillity, they can trank me as much as they like. Aren't I half dead already, and isn't the half that's alive the half that hurts? Go on, finish the job, make me a trank, I won't complain !

As for the other things they can do – well, I wish them luck. They won't allow me any Work Hours? Fine, I'll crawl into a corner and write. Writing's the hardest work I've ever done and the most enjoyable.

If more people knew about writing, we wouldn't have this employment problem. Of *course* people can't be employed more than a few hours a week, of *course* there isn't the work to go round – I admit all that. But if everyone's crying out to be allowed to work, why can't they make their own work instead of going around moaning and ending up plugged into the Viddy?

My mother used to wash her own dishes, I've seen her do it. She used water and some other stuff and as soon as she'd finished washing them she'd wipe each one with a cloth. The Official Authority found out in the end, of course, and stopped it because she was using the same dishes over and over again instead of new ones each time. But she used to love it, she'd hum to herself while she did it.

Anyhow, there must be a hundred work things people could do without being anti-social. My writing doesn't hurt anyone, for example. And if it does, how are they going to stop me doing it? You can write with your fingernail on dust if you have to.

Where was I? Oh yes, I said to Uncle Lipton, 'We've got to go.' Then I said, 'How is it done? What happens?'

He explained it like this. He'd mastered Xtend so that he could think himself through time. At first it had taken him hours, sleepless night after sleepless night. But, at last, he got the time-trek trick by fixing his mind on the time he wanted to visit. I believe some people can wake themselves at any given hour – they bang their head on the pillow eight times and sure enough they wake up at eight ... Anyhow, Uncle Lipton concentrates and concentrates until certain things happen. First, he says, he feels sleepy. Then his legs begin to itch and twitch about, but he doesn't turn over. Apparently this is important, you must keep still. Then he gets a dream or a vision – just a flash – of the time he wants to travel to. 'If I get that, lad – if I see the people actually walking about and if I see things and faces that *surprise* me – then I'm half-way there.' That's the way he put it.

I asked him what happened then and he answered, 'I don't really know, lad. I remember once when I was in the future – it was a century or so ahead, that trip – I saw the people, I got the flash, and I tried to reach out and say something. And I couldn't think of a blind thing to say except, "Can you tell me the time?" At last some blighter turned round and actually listened to me and I was *in*. I'd made it.'

'What did you do then? Did he tell you the time?'

'He just gaped at me. I walked away fast. I didn't want to chance my arm by opening my mouth, if you see what I mean. No, I just lurked about and looked and listened until I knew the form. Must know the form first.'

'Well, what *was* the form?'

Uncle Lipton suddenly glanced sideways, grabbed my arm and said, 'Look, there's a whole cluster of shocking types coming in. Will you come or won't you? And if you do come, will you behave yourself and do what you're told?'

'Yes. Yes, I will. But *how*?'

'Swallow this.' He gave me a pill and I swallowed it. His eyes were swivelling round while I did it. 'And here are two more,' he said, clumsily thrusting two pills into my pocket. 'Seems a dreadful waste, probably won't work on you at all. And perhaps I need them for myself, but too late now ... Take one tonight and don't go to sleep. Stay awake. Think. Think. I'll think too. I'll be *willing* you.'

'What am I to think about?'

'World War II, laddie, World War II, 1939. World War II. Got it? A steam train, a railway station, lots of kids all wearing labels. You're one of the kids, got it?'

I'd got it. I'd seen plenty of pictures of trains and stations in Uncle Lipton's books. The old railways fascinate me. I could easily think the way he wanted. He's a clever old devil in some ways, my Uncle Lipton.

*

I lay awake trying to think the thoughts Uncle Lipton wanted me to think, but it wasn't all that easy. First, I didn't believe it would work and you can't think the right way if you are doubting. Second, I was puzzled by Uncle Lipton wanting me to be among a crowd of kids on a train. I got the answer to that later and it was a clever answer.

Anyhow, I lay awake and lay awake until I had to fall asleep. But just before that happened, I did have a strange feeling. I felt that Uncle Lipton was there beside me, puffing out his cheeks and saying things. I seemed to hear him say, 'Pull yourself together lad, try. Try ! No gumption at all, pull yourself together lad and *try* !'

Next morning, I asked him about this and he said he had been pushing just such thoughts at me. He said, 'I never really expected it to work straight away, lad. And I might as well tell you now it may take weeks, even months. But we'll do it in the end, boy, do it in the end, just trust your Uncle Lipton.'

I thought he was talking nonsense as usual and when I went to bed that night and took another Xtend pill, I said to myself, 'Well, I'll give it a try for half an hour, but that's all.' I lay on my back without moving (usually I sleep on my side) and concentrated very hard on steam trains, lots of children wearing labels and so on. But nothing much happened except that my nose began to itch. You weren't supposed to move, of course. In the end, however, I gave it up, scratched my nose and turned on my right side, ready to sleep.

It was just then that the answer came to me – the answer to Uncle Lipton's funny-sounding plan of starting me on my voyage back in time in a railway carriage, with a lot of kids. Evacuees ! That was the answer, evacuees !

I knew what the word meant, of course. Uncle Lipton had told me about the evacuees. When World War II started, everyone was afraid that the sky would be black with bombers, all raining death and destruction on Britain's men, women and children. So the British government decided to 'evacuate' the children – that is, to send them away from the big cities (particularly London, which was then the biggest city of all – not a burnt-out wasteland, like it is today) and get them into what was called the countryside, that is, the places where there were wide open spaces and farms and villages. The government actually did this, before and during the war. Busloads of kids, all labelled with their names and destinations, were taken to the big railway stations, put on the trains and sent to the countryside, where they would be safe from the bombers.

Uncle Lipton's plan was to plant me in the mix-up of migrant children – because by doing this, no one would question my sudden appearance in the wrong century! I would be one of a huge horde of 'foreigners'. Nobody would take much notice of me. Anything strange or wrong that I did would be excused or overlooked or just not thought about at all.

So there I was, lying on my side and getting ready to go to sleep and thinking how clever Uncle Lipton could be when he wasn't being stupid. I began thinking about the evacuation, wondering how it felt to be a child taken away from its home and put on a train and left to start its little life all over again with strange people in a strange place. It must have been awful for most of them. In those days, remember, people lived in families, not in Homebody Units. There were mums and dads and brothers and sisters – not just the Counsellors and the Viddy playgrounds and all the rest of it. You can feel alone in 2079 (worse luck) – but in 1939, some of the evacuee kids must have suffered terrible fears and loneliness and sadness.

That was what I was thinking about, lying in bed. About the children with the labels in 1939. I was thinking this deeply when, out of nowhere, a nasty squeaky little voice said, 'Ere! Geroff moy bleedin' foot!'

Those were the first twentieth-century words I heard.

*

I didn't understand for a moment, but then I translated it into English. The voice had said, 'Here! Get off my foot!' 'Bleeding' was just an adjective. I moved my foot. She said, 'Bout bleedin' toym.'

She was a horrible little girl. She was dirty. Her nose was dirty and and her teeth were green. She couldn't close her mouth properly, it hung open all the time, that was how I saw her teeth. She had greasy hair. It hung in rat-tails round her dirty face. Here eyes were tough and fierce and fearless as a rat's.

I tried to move away from her but the carriage was too full. There must have been twenty of us in that one dusty little compartment, about twelve or fourteen on the seats and the rest of us swaying and trampling each other in between, standing. The train was going along quite fast. I could hear the steam engine chuffing away and the sound of the wheels on the tracks. The tracks weren't continuous and the wheels made a sort of rhythmic sound pattern on the joins, they went 'Arangadadang, arangadadang'. I could see the telegraph poles going by the windows and the telegraph wires hung between the poles kept swooping and dipping, out of time with the rhythm of the wheels.

I liked all this, I could have looked and listened for ever, but the little girl said, 'Doynow! Fency beig cord Doynow! Wa sortoffer nime is Doynow!'

She'd been reading my name on the label pinned to my lapel. I could understand what she said. 'Dano! Fancy being called Dano! What sort of name is Dano!' It took me time to work this out, though, and by the time I was ready to say something she had turned to a dirty little boy, her brother, and said, 'E's cord Doynow, didjever!' Her name was Shirley Biggs, I read it on her label. The boy was William Albert Biggs. I said, 'Plenty of people are called Dano,' and she yelled, 'Ere! Lissen to 'im! 'E's a bleeding yank, 'e torks Merican!'

All of a sudden the other kids started singing Roll out the

Barrel and I was left alone. I pretended to be singing, but I wasn't. I was listening, trying to pick up the way they spoke. But when the song ended and they started talking again, I realized that they all spoke differently. Take the word 'Dano'. One of the kids would have said 'Doynow', another 'Di-naow', still another 'Dano'. I kept my mouth shut and listened. It was like being in a parrot house, they screeched and yelled and jabbered. Shirley Biggs squatted on the floor and made a puddle, and the other kids said, 'Ooo, int she AW-foo !'

They smelled. Their clothes smelled of damp paper or cloth or something. I can't describe it, it isn't a smell you meet in this century. Their hair smelled. Some of the boys, even the little ones, had their hair smarmed with a thick scented grease and combed into big sweeping waves. The grease was called hair cream, it had a smell all of its own, especially on dirty hair. Sick-sweet.

Their clothes were much thicker and clumsier than ours, especially the boys' clothes. They were made of woollen cloth, wool from sheep, and all the kids wore wool stockings or socks. They had big clumsy shoes with laces in them. The shoes were made of cow-leather. Nearly everything they wore came from animals and the children smelled like animals.

Now you can ask me, did I like them? If I'm so scornful about this century, what was so wonderful about the dirty, smelly kids then?

The answer is, I didn't like them. They made me feel sick, particularly their smell. I didn't like their faces, their voices, their looks, anything. I was afraid of them, too – it was like being put in a zoo cage with wild animals. I didn't like the thick, coarse, twentieth-century clothes I found myself wearing, or the crumpled label, or my creased, heavy, leathery shoes or my itchy socks (they came nearly up to my knees. You had a rubber band in the top, where the socks were turned over, and the rubber band was supposed to keep your socks from falling down. It didn't work, of course).

Well, what *did* I like about them, then? Read on, read on . . .

I won't write any more about the train journey, because it was a mess and not worth writing about. The train stopped, the train started, we got off the train and waited for a motor coach, we got in the coach and waited, we sang *Roll out the Barrel*, we got out of the coach and waited and sang *Why are we Waiting?* It was just like today, in fact, except that the hardware was cruder. You did what the Official Authority told you to do and it took far too long.

But I will write about the *way* we did what we were told. We moaned all the time. We moaned and jeered and wanted to Be Excused. Shirley Biggs always wanted to be excused, though she couldn't have had anything to be excused with after about the fortieth time. We were horrible to anyone our own size and nice to anyone very much smaller – one girl, I don't know her name, took care of a little girl who wouldn't stop crying. When the Official Authority people took the little girl away, smiling, the big girl started crying and we yelled and gave them the Nazi salute (you stick out your right arm at forty-five degrees, up in the air, and shout 'Heil Hitler').

We fought *everything* – each other, the Official Authority, the tea with too much sugar in it, the tea with too little sugar – *everything*. Perhaps now you'll begin to understand why I liked being with the twentieth-century kids. They were alive and kicking, not dead and docile.

At last, the whole trainload of us was broken down into groups. It took all day. We were put into motor coaches or another train or even cars and taxis. I was one of the last to go, my name wasn't on the lists, so I went with two girls, Madelaine Evans and Jackie Morton. The three of us shuffled forward with our suitcases in our hands and our gas masks (I'll tell you more about gas masks later) in their little square cardboard boxes strung over our shoulders. I was tired, but not too tired to be grateful that Shirley and William Albert Biggs weren't on our list.

'These are the ones for Halpington Farm,' said a worried-looking woman.

'That's my lot, then,' a man said. 'Get in the Rolls and mind you don't scratch the paint.'

The man's name was Arthur. He was a farmer, a big, brown, strong, happy man with very white false teeth.

The 'Rolls' was a two-wheeled trailer half filled with straw, hitched to an Austin Heavy 12 – a solid old saloon car. The back of the car was filled with farm gear so we had to go in the trailer. It was quite comfortable, we had the straw to lie on and mess about with.

The old Austin's gears crunched and grated and growled and we were off. I saw for the first time the world that existed before World War III. A wide-open world. Yet to Arthur and most other country people, I found out later, it was little or nothing. The sudden golden ochre of a ripening field, the hedgerow plants reaching out to tickle you, the great wrinkled trees to climb and the little unlined trees so slow and steady in growing, the tawny-roofed farmhouse winking its sly windows at you, the mild sheep in the wide meadow, the horses wanting to know where we were going and galumping along behind the hedge to keep up with the slow old Austin – all these things were nothing to Arthur, he just chucked his fag end at them and rolled on, whistling through his lovely false teeth.

We had almost got there – to the farmhouse, to Halpington Farm – before I looked at the other kids. I was going to spend I didn't know how long with them, so it was about time to have a good look.

Madelaine Evans was six, I think, or perhaps seven. Mad was pretty in a rolypoly way. Her hair – it was dark blonde – curled. All of her curled. She had a curly mind, a curl at the corner of her mouth when she smiled. That evening when we were reaching Halpington Farm she was tired out, but she still kept the old curl going somehow. She was singing *I wish I could shimmy like my sister Kate, she wobbles like jelly on a plate*. She was singing this song to herself, quietly and curlily.

Jackie Morton was a big-sister sort of girl from Ealing, a suburb of London. She was the sort of girl who does well at school. She must have been ten. I suppose she was all right, I liked her, it's just that I don't remember her very well. She was very plain, her hair was dark and no particular colour. It just grew out of her head and fell down straight, like blinds on either side of her face. Sometimes she wore a celluloid hair slide to keep the blinds back. She was tall and strong for her age and a good worker.

When we got to the farmhouse, there was nobody to meet us. I was a bit surprised, but Arthur wasn't. He said, 'She'll be milking, rackon.' 'She' was his wife, Florence, but he called her Flo. Arthur always said 'rackon'. It meant 'I reckon'.

We all went inside, Arthur carrying the cases and gas masks. You probably wouldn't have liked the main room because there was so much space, but I liked it straight away. There was a gingery upright piano that nobody ever played, covered with family photographs; a long table with food on it; a fireplace with logs waiting to be lit and a mantelpiece above it with ugly vases and pretty flowers – and more photographs. There were dark, dusty curtains with big wooden rings, dark dusty wallpaper, rugs, dogs, battered armchairs, uncomfortable wooden chairs at the table.

Mad said, 'I'm hungry !' – grinned – and sat down and ate. She looked very small in the big chair but she could eat all right. I found that I could eat quite a lot too. We had hot soup, cold ham, cold chicken, salad, cheese, pickles and lemonade made from yellow crystals.

We saw the farmhouse properly next day. It was a lovely mess. The actual house was a plain-faced grey box with big white windows and a fanlight over the front door, what they called a Georgian house. It was small and looked even smaller because it was swamped by the other buildings. At right angles to it there was a barn, made partly of flint and partly of dark brown creosoted wood. Where the wood had gone rotten, Arthur had stuck up a big enamelled sign for Oakshott Cattle Cakes. There was a picture of a cow and lots of other writing on this sign telling you how many medals Oakshott Cakes had won.

At the back of the house there were well-built stalls and stables, in flint, where the horses lived. The cows were somewhere else. The three horses were called Mabel, Tinker and Harry Boy. Harry Boy was the best, he'd let you do anything and never complain. The cows all had names too. There were eighteen cows and I knew all their names and could recognize every one of them miles away within a week. I won't tell you all their names, just the best – Pansy, Violet, Buttercup, Bonny, Little Flo (after Arthur's wife as she had delivered this particular cow), Marie and Dirty Gertie – she was all black.

There were all sorts of other buildings and bits of buildings. There was a place where Arthur's unmarried brother George grew mushrooms. It was a cellar with a broken barn leaning over it. The smell in the cellar was frightening, but the mushrooms were delicious. We had them fried for breakfast. And there was a little dairy, where the milk was cooled and put into churns. That was cold yet fresh.

The best building was a railway carriage. It was at the far end of the garden. Arthur was very proud of it. He said it was the best hen-house a man could have – it would last and last because 'the wood was proper coach-varnished'. The funny thing was, that he never kept any poultry in it.

Now, when I began writing this bit, I described Arthur as a big, strong, happy man.

Was Arthur big? Yes. The average height of a man today

is five foot four inches. Arthur stood just under six feet tall.

Was he strong? Yes. He used to lift Mad and me up, one in each hand, just like that, straight off the ground. But that was nothing. I've seen him lift the back end of a farm cart when it nearly rolled over a piglet.

Ah, but was he happy? Yes, but of course you can't believe me. You're always running to the Counsellor, aren't you? 'Oh, Counsellor! I'm so unhappy!'

'What is it, Homebody number three million and three? Why are you unhappy?'

'Because I'm unhappy about the unhappy possibility of being unhappy, Counsellor.'

'I quite understand, Homebody number three million and three. Now just you lie down on that nice shiny couch, and let's see your tummy button. . . . *That's* it . . .' And into your navel pops the jackplug, round go the dials, up goes the happiness rating.

'Don't forget now!' cries the Counsellor when you're disconnected. 'Stay tuned! Stay happy! I'm always here!' And off you trot, tra la la, and that night the Viddy's never been so good nor the bevvie so delicious. Fantass, fantass, fantass! Any time, any time at all!

It wasn't like that for Arthur. He was a naturally happy man. He suited himself and his wife and his children. He didn't need to get tuned. He didn't even have anywhere for the jackplug to go in – his navel had nothing in it but fluff.

People in 2079 moan about work because they haven't any. Arthur used to moan about work because he had too much. He used to work and work and work, often more than twelve hours a day. He even worked when he was ill. Hard to imagine, isn't it?

Mad – Madelaine – was the one I liked best. She made me laugh. You never knew what she was going to say, she said the maddest things. She came into the bathroom when I was washing – I think it was the very morning the pilot came down – and said, 'I think I have some muscles.' Then she flexed her arm, white on the inside and brown on the outside, and sure enough there was a little bump on the bicep part of of it. Hardly a bump, just a curve. She made me feel it and I laughed at her, it felt like nothing. The thing was, that she was half laughing too.

On this particular day, when the pilot came down, I took Mad with me when I went to see the corporal. We called him Corp. He was on the searchlight site by the sea, he more or less lived there. There was a little Nissen hut, lots of sandbags round the light, some camouflage netting and quite often a truck. The truck brought food to the corporal and the soldiers who manned the light and the soldiers who worked the detector gear nearby that picked up the sound of the enemy aircraft. Sometimes there were only three men on the site, sometimes half a dozen, but the corporal always seemed to be there. Whenever we saw him, he seemed to be 'brewing up' – that is, making tea. He never stopped brewing up. He'd see us coming and say, 'Yerss. You again.' We said nothing. When he'd made his tea, he'd say, 'None for you, nor her neither. Tea's rationed.' Then he'd give us great tin mugs of it.

He was probably the ugliest man I have ever seen. He had a smashed nose, no neck, a grating voice and always needed a shave. He wore gumboots. I think he must have been born in gumboots.

That day, the day of the pilot, Mad went straight up to him and said, 'Go on! Sing a fiffy song!' When she said 'fiffy' she meant 'filthy'. She had heard some women in the village say, 'Oh, those disgusting soldiers, singing filthy songs!' and Mad wanted to know more.

Corp said, 'All right. Yerss . . .' and began to sing straight away. His singing was like a dog growling. He sang:

> 'Hurrah for Betox! What a delightful smell!
> The stuff that every self-respecting grocer has
> to sell!

The price is right, it's cook's delight,
How easily it's made –
So join the happy families of the Betox
    Brigade !'

Mad said, 'Was that song fiffy?' She looked doubtful. The
Corp growled, 'Yerss. 'Orrible,' and she cheered up. Betox was
stuff you cooked with. So even in those days they had com-
mercials. But they didn't have the Viddy, it was just on the
radio. They didn't even have television, which came before
the Viddy.

Mad wanted Corp to teach her his song. He was just starting when we heard the machine guns.

If I was a liar I would make something really dramatic out
of the air fights and the machine guns, but I will tell you the
truth. What was happening was this : the Germans wanted
to invade England and to do that they had to get control of
the air. Once they'd got control of the air, the British
wouldn't be able to stop the Germans' invasion barges from
crossing the English Channel. The Germans would have
bombed England, bombed and machine-gunned anything that
tried to stop the invasion barges – and then the Germans
would have landed their troops on the beaches and the English wouldn't have been able to hold them back.

That was the idea. Where it went wrong was that the
Germans couldn't win the air battle. They should have been
able to but they couldn't. The British Spitfire and Hurricane
fighter aircraft kept shooting down the German fighters and
bombers so the Germans couldn't invade.

Anyhow, we used to see quite a lot of this battle of the
British aircraft against the Germans, the 'Battle of Britain'.
The Germans would fly over the coast; the English radar
stations would detect them as they flew and send out the
alarm; the British fighters would take off; and then there
would be a fight in the sky between the two sides. As I say,
these battles ought to have been very dramatic but they
weren't really, whatever you've seen on the Viddy. All you

could see from the ground – we saw it quite often – was little tiny dots in the sky a long way up, circling round each other. Sometimes there would be white trails in the blue sky. Sometimes you could hear a sort of hollow, tinny, rattling sound from a long way away. That sound was the machine guns.

This particular day, we could see and hear the warplanes fighting up in the sky and hear the machine guns. Then something happened that really was dramatic. Two of the little dots suddenly became balls of fire! One of the fireballs just sort of broke up into nothing, it made a spider web of bits of aircraft with thin black smoke trailing away as the bits fell. The other fireball turned into an aircraft. It came spiralling down, down and down, with a great trail of black smoke behind it. We were all quiet because we didn't know if the aircraft was ours or theirs.

Then the other dramatic thing happened. We saw a little black dot in the sky suddenly make a silvery white dot. We knew what this was, of course. It was the pilot's parachute. It came closer and closer, this parachute and we could see the pilot hanging on to it. He looked tiny. Soon he looked bigger and then bigger still. He seemed to be coming towards us!

Mad said, 'He'll hit my head,' and put her hands over her head to keep the pilot out of her hair.

He came lower and lower and the Corp got his rifle and stood there for a minute working the bolt and making sure it was loaded. Then he started walking away. I said, 'Where are you going, Corp?' He said, 'Over there. He'll come down over there.' After a time, he started running. He kept looking back over his shoulder, then he'd make up his mind and start running again.

I didn't think the Corp was right. I thought the pilot would come down not behind us, but in front of us. So I started running in the opposite direction and Mad yelled out, 'Wait for me!' but I didn't. She hopped about a bit and then ran after Corp.

But I was right. The pilot and his parachute were coming

down where I thought they would, not where Corp thought they would. I ran so hard that I thought my nose would bleed. Because, by now, the pilot was quite close to the ground. I could see him perfectly. His head was hanging down.

He hit the ground with a sort of slack, rotten bump, it made me feel frightened to see it. He fell forward, right on his face. I ran up to him.

You've never seen so much blood. It was pouring out of his arm, pumping out. He'd been hit by a machine-gun bullet, up in the sky. I was terrified of the blood, there was so much of it. I wasn't frightened of him at all, he was just a young-looking blond man. I didn't know what to do. But then he moved and made a noise, he looked up at the sky and tried to sit up. Then he said some words. They weren't in English so I knew he must be a German.

He managed to sit up and started twisting his sleeve against his arm. He was trying to stop the bleeding. Then he noticed me for the first time and said something to me. The blood was dripping down his arm under his clothes and pouring on to the grass over his hand and fingers. I just had to do something. I got out my handkerchief, which was all dirty, and twisted and knotted it to make a ring, and gave it to the German. He grabbed it and twisted it round his arm, then started looking around.

I knew what he wanted – a stick. I started running about and soon found a good strong stick and I gave it to him. He made a tourniquet with the stick and the handkerchief and said, 'Ja, ja. Ja, ja.' Then just when he'd got the tourniquet right, he fell over sideways in the grass and the tourniquet came undone and the blood started again.

I didn't want the German to die, I wanted to help him. I grabbed the stick and twisted it until the tourniquet tightened up. You could see the blood slow down, it didn't keep pumping out any more, so I knew I was doing it right. I knelt there for quite a long time holding on to the stick. I remember I was half frightened to look at the German and all the blood so I looked to one side of him. I remember seeing a little flower we called Egg and Bacon deep down in the grass, and a bumble bee.

Then Corp came up, puffing and blowing. He had run a mile or more, first the wrong way, then back again, then my way, so he was out of breath. He said, "Un', meaning that the pilot was a Hun, a German. He pointed his rifle at the pilot, but then gave up and knelt down beside him. I said, 'He's badly wounded,' and Corp said, 'Yerss.' The pilot kept saying, 'Danke,' to me whenever he was well enough. 'Danke' means 'Thanks'.

In the end, some other soldiers came along from a truck and we didn't see the pilot again for about two months. His fighter plane landed miles away.

Now you'll want to ask me a question, won't you? You'll want to ask, 'Didn't you remember Uncle Lipton's warning about interfering with history? Didn't you think you were doing something dangerous and wrong when you got the stick and retightened the tourniquet? Shouldn't you have let the German die?'

The answers are, I *did* remember Uncle Lipton's warning but I *couldn't* let the man die. I bet you couldn't either.

But you certainly asked the right question. And if you think the answer affects the rest of this story, you're right again.

We saw Axel – that turned out to be the pilot's name – again two months or so after he'd been shot down. It was late summer, harvest time. We kids had to go out in the fields and work with the villagers. Nearly everyone was out in the fields for the harvest, it was the most important time of the year. A lot of the work was done by weird old machines that clanked and rattled and jiggled and squeaked. There were horses and steam engines to pull this and drive that. But most of the work was done by humans. You had to keep at it, you never thought to stop because that would be 'cissy'.

I worked so hard that I soon forgot about my German pilot. But one day – it was after the thrashing – there he was, standing by the gate of the five-acre field, watching us working.

They'd patched him up in hospital, but he still had one leg in plaster and his ribs were bandaged (his arm wasn't bad at all, it soon healed). His whole leg was in plaster, there was a sort of steel hoop sticking out at the bottom so he could hobble about without spoiling the plaster. You've never heard of plaster? To mend bones in those days, they used to wrap the broken bit up with a white clay that set solid so the broken bone couldn't move and therefore mended of its own accord. The ostografts we use today hadn't been invented.

So there was Axel with an enormous white leg. He couldn't have escaped if he had wanted to. He was, of course, a prisoner of war – a PoW as they called it – and should have been kept in a sort of prison. But the British were soft about that sort of thing. They let Axel out because he was not the escaping type and also because he was a whizz mechanic. We were told that he had mended appliances in the hospital (in the twentieth century, surgery was literally a matter of sawing and cutting and drilling and they had a lot of complicated machines).

Axel was good with the farm machines too. He couldn't handle them himself, you could tell he was a brains type (what they called a boffin); but he could just take one look at a clock or a tractor or anything else and say, 'Ja, ja, ve vill make it to work.' He couldn't pronounce his Ws, many Germans could not.

We kids tried to talk to him. At first we thought he must be a murderous fascist beast but we very soon learned that he wasn't that at all. He was quite simply a cold fish. He was just like the people of today, all discipline and training and conformity. But he was also somebody who really could think.

Talking with him was very difficult because he didn't speak much English and we spoke no German. But what Axel couldn't speak, he could do. For instance, if we tried to talk about aeroplanes to him, he would grope about for the right words, then give up and sit down and *make* an aeroplane for us instead of talking. When I say make an aeroplane, I mean just that. He'd take rubber bands and tissue paper and little bits of wood and wire and next thing you'd know – look up there, it's flying! He could make tanks out of cotton reels, matchsticks, candle ends, rubber bands and bent wire. They'd climb up cushions and over earth. He could mend bicycle three-speed gears and dynamos and toy steam engines. He could even make yo-yo strings, the ones that let the yo-yo spin so that you could do Walking the Dog and Round the World (if I've lost you, ask the Viddy. No, don't bother, even Viddy won't be able to tell you about yo-yos).

So we got to like Axel. Well, not like, but rely on. He was not likeable, really. But fascinating because of the huge brain and abilities. Even we kids could see what an amazing man he was.

One day I asked him what he was going to do when the war was over. He started mumbling, 'Ven ... var ... enden, then must I ...' but then gave up and started making aeroplane movements with his hands. I said, 'Aircraft? Aeroplanes?' He said, 'Nein, nein, not so ...' Then he started making whooshing noises with his mouth while waggling his hands about like an aircraft. He managed to get it across to us, he was going to make rockets. Rockets were the thing. 'Rockets!' he said, 'Ja, rockets! Ven var enden, aeroplane kaput ... Rockets, rockets! Whoosh!' And he pointed right up into the sky, jabbing his clean, bony, blond finger at the sun, jabbing it higher still. Space rockets.

I remember so well him doing this. All you need remember is this: Axel's second name was Stern. Axel Stern. *The* Axel Stern. It was Axel Stern, as you know, who was directly responsible for the pioneer space flights in the second half of the twentieth century.

And it was Axel Stern whose inventions made possible the attempted flight to the Galaxy. My Uncle Lipton owes all he is – or isn't – today, to Axel Stern.

When I started this book, almost the first words I wrote were about circular insanity, do you remember? Well, let's get back to that thought and I'll show you just how circularly insane we've got.

The story so far : long ago, before I was born, Uncle Lipton went on the spaceshot to the Galaxy. He took the keep-young drug Xtend so that he would arrive at the Galaxy still a young man. If there hadn't been a Galaxy spaceshot, the scientists might never have invented Xtend. If they hadn't invented Xtend, Uncle Lipton would be dead and buried long ago and I would never have known him.

All right so far? Hold tight and we'll go further.

Because of Uncle Lipton, I was able to travel back through time. Because I travelled back through time, I was there when Axel Stern baled out with his parachute. Because I stopped Axel Stern bleeding to death, he lived.

And then what happened? Axel Stern, German pilot, became Axel Stern, spacecraft inventor and pioneer. It was Axel Stern, more than any other man, who got Uncle Lipton into space, heading for the Galaxy.

Now you can see where the circular insanity is coming in. But I'll spell it out for you anyway . . .

I wasn't even born when Axel Stern should have bled to death after his dogfight. Yet I saved Axel Stern from bleeding to death.

Uncle Lipton went on the Galaxy spaceshot only because a man who should have been dead was saved by a boy who hadn't yet been born.

Xtend was invented to preserve life during spaceshots; however, Xtend might never have been invented if Axel

Stern hadn't lived. But then, if Xtend hadn't been invented, I wouldn't have been able to travel back through time. And if I hadn't been able to travel back, Axel Stern would have died and there might have been no need for anyone to invent Xtend.

I like that last paragraph, I really do. The more you read it, the less sense it makes.

And that's what I mean by circular insanity.

Anyhow, there I was on the farm, completely happy, happy as I'd never been before and never will be again. I never thought about today, the twenty-first century. I never thought about Viddy, or Homebody Units, or Uncle Lipton.

But one day I was forced to think of him. There was a beep-beep from one of those little grey RAF Hillman saloons; the WAAF girl driver opened its little rear door; and out stepped Uncle Lipton.

It wouldn't be true to say I hardly recognized him – you couldn't fail to recognize the bottle-nosed old bounder – but I must have blinked once or twice, or pinched myself, or done something to make myself believe it was he. He looked so well, so blooming, so prosperous. The old half show-off, half furtive manner was gone. Now he was completely show-off, from his rakish check golfing cap down to his beautifully polished weathered brown brogues. I remember that between these two ends of him, there was a silk foulard neck scarf pulled through a gold ring, a houndstooth check shooting jacket with great big vents, silver grey flannel trousers and a pale blue RAF Officer-quality shirt. I remember the shirt particularly : the cuffs were actually clean.

'Tally-ho !' he roared, waving a knobbly walking stick at me. 'Tally-ho, chaps ! Bandits at –' he pointed the stick at me and cocked an eye at the sun –'230. Attack !' He went on waffling in RAF fighter-pilot talk, getting it all wrong, while he seized my hand in his great paw and pumped it up and down. 'Well, well, well!' he said. 'Well, well, well! Me old winger Dano!'

I was red in the face before he came, we had been trying to get a coulter off a plough and it wouldn't come, the bolts were rusted. I felt myself going red under the redness all the same. I didn't know what to say. I looked up at Arthur, who was with me and the plough, and he gave a little nod that meant I could slink off with my visitor. So I slunk.

He'd only come to show off, Uncle Lipton. It turned out that he had been made catering manager of the biggest RAF station in Kent. It was a civilian job, he had to see to all the food and drink supplies. I could see why he got the job, he was just the sort of old villain who'd be able to lay his hands on scarce foods and drinks. You could judge his success by smelling his breath. Even the piglets seemed to flinch a bit when he inspected them. Or perhaps they knew him to be the sort of man who pokes pigs with his stick. He did a lot of expert stick-poking, of course. He knew everything about farming, except that he knew nothing at all.

It took a long time to get down to business.

'Uncle,' I said, 'what's happening while we're away? What will they be thinking?'

'About me?' he replied. 'Nothing. Glad to be rid of me. Anyhow, I've disappeared before.'

'And about me?'

'Yes, there's you,' he said, biting his lower lip. I forgot to tell you that he had grown one of those great bushy RAF moustaches, about nine inches across. When he bit his lip, it looked like a badger digging a tunnel.

'Freaked out,' he said at last, 'took your skimmer and freaked out. Happens all the time. Simple.'

'But I don't freak, they know that,' I said. 'I'm not graded for freaking.'

'Well, tell 'em you *did*,' he said. 'Everyone's got to start some time, and this was your time.'

I thought about this and didn't like it. There were the

complications of the skimmer – all the skimmers were registered and issued with autotrackers, but that wasn't too difficult, freakouts just broke the trackers up and then their skimmers couldn't be traced.

'I could say I'd turned natural,' I said.

'Bang on!' said Uncle Lipton. 'Wizard wheeze! You went natural, and that's how you got your hands like that. Big walk-about in the wilds, living on berries and herbs –'

'There aren't any berries and herbs back there,' I said. All the same, people did leave their unit and go natural. Some of them kept it up for a week and more. But they always gave up when their food ran out – there was no question of living off the badlands so as soon as they got hungry, they came crawling back. On the other hand, I had often thought of going natural properly – loading the skimmer with food, ditching the skimmer, making a food cache, living in a cave. Doing it for weeks, not just days. Perhaps I could fool the Official Authority with a story based on that old dream?

Then another idea struck me. 'Suppose I *don't* go back?' I asked Uncle Lipton.

'I tried it once, lad. Let things slide for months, couldn't face the bind of going back. Got very complicated, people asked questions. And there were changes, physical changes. Long stretches of blankness, sort of, when I couldn't do anything –'

'Were you drinking at the time?' I said.

He glared at me and said, 'None of your bloody business. In point of fact, I was pretty well sloshed most of the time, but I've had more barrelfuls than you've had hot dinners, so I know what to expect.'

He went on in a different tone. 'No, lad, it wasn't drink. It was a sort of haze, a trance. Between two worlds, that's the phrase I'm groping for. You come to feel that you're between two worlds. You know your time is up, know you've got to go back. I can't tell you how, but you know all right.'

I couldn't think of any reply. I looked about me. In the

six-acre, Arthur was doing something to a stack. It was a good tight stack but he always worried about them. I guessed he was tightening the tarpaulin. And I could see Mad come out of the dairy and go into the farm. She was miles away, but I knew it was her and I could suddenly feel in my hands the blue jug she was carrying, the jug used for cream. I could see the cream and the little crack near the jug's lip. I couldn't make my mind concentrate on anything but the farm, I couldn't think of the future, only of now.

Uncle Lipton left a few minutes later, waving his stick and jollying the WAAF driver. He left in glory, shouting out of the little car he had somehow fiddled, despite RAF regulations and petrol regulations.

And I went back to the farm and my real life. Uncle Lipton had no part in it, I thought.

I thought wrong.

My real life. That's how I'd come to regard the farm and Mad and Arthur and the Corp – and Pansy, Violet and Dirty Gertie. Even the cows and the old enamelled tin sign about the Cow Cakes: these were my real life.

Didn't I think about Homebody Unit 362, you ask? Well, I did, in a way. Sometimes that life would flash at me suddenly, when I was walking down a lane or falling asleep or helping Arthur to shovel muck. One minute I'd be thinking how hard and dark my arms had become (this was during the muck-shovelling, let's say) and admiring all the muscles jumping about under the brown, scratched skin: and the next minute, while I was looking at them, the same arms would be all of a sudden dressed in crapelon Smoosilk and holding a cup of Bevvie. I'd have a flash, a sort of vision, of 2079, the time I'd come from. A flash like that could spoil the rest of the day for me.

Well, now I seemed to be getting them more often. And something worse. I'll describe it.

One of the things we used to like doing in the evenings

was having little concerts. You wouldn't have liked them, they were nothing like Viddy, but we thought they were marvellous because we were doing them.

'Go on, Jackie, your turn now!' we'd shout and Jackie – you remember her, she was the quiet, motherly one, the one who cleared up after us and never complained – Jackie would go all red and fold her arms across her chest and drop her head forward so that her hair hid her face. But in the end, she'd fetch her glockenspiel – a little portable xylophone with tin notes that you hit with mallets. She'd put it on the table and we'd push aside all the plates and cheese and pickles to make room. Concerts happened after dinner, of course. There was no time for playing about during the day.

'Go on, Jackie! *Red Sails in the Sunset! Give us that!'*

And Jackie would pick the tune out, you could see her lips going 'One-two-three-four' to keep the beat. She could play *Red Sails in the Sunset, Bless this House, Pop goes the Weasel,* and the first bit of *In the Mood.* She could do *God Save the King* too, but we always saved that till last and all joined in.

Anyhow, we'd all keep quiet as a mouse, just watching and listening and nodding our heads in time while she did a tune all by herself. She didn't like doing it and yet she did, if you understand what I mean, so we had to be quiet for her. When she finished we'd all clap and Arthur would say, 'First rate, rackon!' and chuckle away to himself.

By now, Mad would be jumping up and down in her chair calling, 'Me! It's me next!' but Flo, Arthur's wife, would wink and say, 'No thank you, madam, you wait your turn. Now, Arthur! . . .'

And he'd get up, beaming, and roaring HURRR! HURRR! to clear his throat, and he'd suddenly bellow out the first lines of a song: *There was a maiden pure as snow, Until she met the vicar* –

And Flo would look shocked and say, 'Oo, Arthur! How dare you! And in front of the children!'

And he'd look all innocent, popping his eyes open wide as they would go. And Flo would frown and we'd all laugh and shout and call, 'Go on, Arthur, I dare you!' but of course he never did. I don't think there really was any more of that song, it was just what they called play-acting.

Anyhow, after that, he'd start singing properly. Only he couldn't sing at all. He'd say to Jackie, 'Give us a note then, love,' and she'd go *Bong* on her glockenspiel. Arthur would look serious and attentive, then open his mouth and let out a note, then nod his head in a satisfied sort of way. But the note he sang was never the *Bong* note, it was miles off. We never let on, we used to burst ourselves trying not to laugh and Flo would look round the table in a resigned sort of way, sharing the joke. She'd say, 'Quiet, children, let's hear Arthur,' and he'd let rip with one of his songs.

He had three. They were *Hush, hush, hush, Here Comes the Bogey Man*; and *With Her Head Tucked Underneath her Arm, She Walks the Bloody Tower*; and *Daddy Wouldn't Buy me a Bow Wow*. You wouldn't know any of them, but I can hear every note and word, in Arthur's voice; and see his face singing too. The thing about the songs was that you all had to join in. You had to whisper, '*Hush ... hush ... hush!*' – or bang the table with your fists for '*With her head* – BANG – *tucked* – BANG – *underneath her arm*' – or do the Bow Wow chorus which went '*Daddy wouldn't buy me a Bow Wow* – (BOW WOW!)'

So those were the songs he sang and once he'd got started, he seemed to keep in tune all right. If he wandered off, Flo would join in and get him back in tune again. She had a nice voice, a really pretty voice somehow. It was tuneful and shy-sounding – yet she wasn't the least bit shy of singing, you might hear her singing at any time. I used to keep quite still, hidden away, when she was working in the dairy because then she'd sing to herself and there must have been something about the milk that she liked because her voice sounded better than ever then. She always sang Christmas carols in the dairy, even in summer.

Then Mad would sing *Animal Crackers in my Soup, Lions and Tigers Loop the Loop.* She'd roll her eyes and pretend to tap dance, like a sort of mad Shirley Temple – that was a little girl film star. Mad hated her because Shirley Temple was so clever and cute. She'd go on and on until we stopped her, always imitating someone. She'd sing *The Lambeth Walk,* strutting round the table with her elbows stuck out. She just wouldn't stop.

In the end, Flo would say, 'That's enough now, surely! I've never seen such a little madam!'

Then it might be my turn. The song I liked best was an old song even in those days. This particular evening, I stood up and started to sing it. *I'm a broken-hearted milkman, in grief I'm arrayed, through keeping of, the company of, a young serving maid.*

I'd got just that far when it happened again – the flash or vision or whatever you like to call it. Suddenly I wasn't there at the farm any more: I wasn't in 2079 either: I was *lost.* Things were flickering. I was lost in time and space.

It seems that I stood there with my mouth open – Jackie told me this after – and I swayed first one way then another, then I fell over.

They got me up to bed. I didn't say or do anything odd. I'd just stopped like an old watch. I stared at nothing. I lay in bed for half an hour or so with Flo beside me, then I came to.

I stared at her face but it seemed out of place in the Bevvie Lounge, which is where I thought I was. Then, clear as anything, I heard Uncle Lipton's voice.

'Time's up, laddie,' he said, right in my ear. 'Time's up, laddie!'

The very next morning, there he was at the farm. He got

out of the little RAF Hillman, walked over to me and said, 'Time's up, laddie.'

I said, 'It can't be, there's no need –'

'We've got to go.'

I could feel the tears pricking my eyes and I was nearly choking. I said, 'I can't! I won't!'

The WAAF driver of the little car shouted, 'Come on, let's get cracking, I've got to be at Group in thirty-five minutes!' The way she said this, I could tell that she didn't think much of Uncle Lipton. And he confirmed this feeling. 'Time's up for me too, you know, laddie,' he said. 'Spot of bother back at the Station. Expecting trouble about the mess accounts.'

'I can't. I won't.'

'You will, laddie, you will. And pretty damn quick. You blanked out last night, didn't you? About nine o'clock? Well, I've been having some funny turns too. You can't fight it, laddie. Time's up.'

'I wish you'd stop calling me "laddie",' I shouted. But I knew he was right and that my life was finished.

The WAAF girl started the car's engine and blew its tinny little horn. 'Are you bloody coming?' she yelled. 'Because I'm bloody going!'

'Bloody go, then!' bellowed Uncle Lipton, suddenly furious and scarlet.

She said, 'You got a date back at the Station – the C.O. wants to see you, you can't –'

Uncle Lipton roared, 'Bloody go, go, GO!' She shrugged and the little car lurched and bumped out of sight.

'A walk, laddie – sorry, I meant Dano,' he said quietly. 'We're going for a walk together. Where's it quiet?' He was very solemn.

As he spoke, I felt it again – another lurch into nothingness. It was over as soon as it began, but I felt it all right, felt the fluttering, tumbling, flickering feeling.

I pointed down the lane without saying anything and we

began to walk down it. After a little while, I started crying and couldn't stop. We walked on past the cows and I could see Dinah the oldest one was in a temper, she was lashing her tail at the flies, but none of the cows took any notice of me. They didn't care that my heart was breaking. And it was breaking, I swear it was, as we walked down that lane.

'In here, Dano,' said Uncle Lipton, very quietly. He pushed me into the trees and bushes round Claypole's pond. The pond hadn't been any good for years, Arthur told me, and it was drying up now. There was a pram handle sticking out of the water and you could see a bit more of the half-sunk tractor tyre every day. The flies and midges were buzzing about but I just let them sting me. I wanted to die.

'Sit down, laddie,' said Uncle Lipton. Then, almost in a whisper, 'Lie down.'

I lay down beside him on the scenty grass and he took my hand. By now, I was hiccoughing as well as crying and my nose was running. He gave me a handkerchief and told me to blow my nose. He kept on at me until I'd blown it properly, then he crumpled up the handkerchief and threw it away. 'Won't be needing *that*,' he said and there was something so dead and hopeless in his voice that I felt pity for him and forgot my own misery for a moment.

'What was it like for you, Uncle?' I asked him.

'Same thing as usual, lad,' he said. 'Dropped a clanger or two. Be a nasty prang if I stayed on. And I've had my dizzy spell too, so we can't stay on. You know that.'

His hand tightened on mine. 'Lie back, Dano,' he said. 'Close your eyes. Close your eyes. Close them tight. Lie back, Dano. Back. Back. Back . . .'

We went back.

They were ready for us.

Earlier, I mentioned World War II gas masks and promised I'd explain about them later. Now is exactly the right time. A gas mask was a smelly rubber face mask with a flexible mica panel to look out of and a tin-can filter, with holes in it, dangling in front of your mouth and chin. You put the whole thing over your face and straps held it there. If the enemy dropped poison gas, the mask was supposed to filter out the poison.

Everyone was instructed to carry their gas masks. Some people in towns actually did, but in the country you never bothered with them until an Air Raid Warden came round and made you put your mask on, just to make sure that you still had it and it was in working order.

When you put the mask on, you had several strange sensations.

First, the flexible mica panel misted up so that you couldn't see properly.

Second, you found it very difficult to breathe.

Third, you had a terrific desire to tear the thing off and get back to normal.

Although I wasn't wearing a gas mask, all these sensations happened to me when I lay beside Uncle Lipton on the bank of Claypole's pond and we began to depart from the 1940s and return to 2079. I was blinded not only by my own tears, but also by a sort of mist as we slipped from one time to another.

I found it difficult to breathe, not only because of the great swelling sorrow in my heart which I thought would burst my chest, but also because the flight through time seemed somehow to stop my body – to check my heart, stifle my lungs, numb my brain.

Above all, I wanted to 'tear the thing off' and 'get back to normal' – in other words, to get back to the real me, my real life, on the farm. I was filled with a huge despair, a hopeless longing.

So now you know about gas masks and time trekking and good-byes and we needn't go into that any more. I will tell you instead about the second experience that reminded me of gas masks.

*

It began with our Homebody Counsellor coming up to me in the Bevvie Lounge. She is a very pretty blonde woman, about thirty, with large, lovely, unintelligent eyes. I was drinking NuChoc, sitting in a chair. I felt her light, friendly touch on my shoulder and heard her smooth, sweet voice (just like NuChoc) say, 'Well, you're back, Dano! Welcome home!'

I said nothing. I just humped my shoulder a little to let her know that I would rather she took her hand away. But she didn't.

'Anything to tell me, Dano?' she purred.

I said nothing.

'Nothing to tell me, Dano? Nothing at all? No explanations?'

I said nothing.

'You're quite sure, Dano?'

I said something very rude that I used to hear the soldiers say. I was trying to think what she could do next.

'All right, Dano,' she said – and I felt a sudden frozen pricking in my shoulder, a tiny sensation. She lifted her hand from my shoulder. 'Quite all right, Dano,' she said. 'Follow me to my office in exactly ten minutes.'

I said the same rude thing again. Follow her in ten minutes! Not likely! I sipped my NuChoc and wondered what to do next. Somehow, I couldn't make my mind work. I couldn't reason, or keep hold of a thought. But at last, I had the complete and perfect solution. Congratulating myself on my cleverness, I got to my feet – walked to the door – and, exactly ten minutes from the time she had left me, I was standing at the Counsellor's little desk reciting my name, description, Homebody Unit number and all the rest of it.

The frozen pricking in my shoulder was spreading. It felt very nice indeed, very comforting, very soothing. I think I told the Counsellor that she was pretty, the prettiest Counsellor of all. I think I remember the Trank Unit people coming in, smiling; and the Counsellor smiling; and no doubt I was smiling too, as they took me away.

I don't remember much else. I suppose I got the full treatment in the Unit. I was a Trank for about six months, doing all the things Tranks do – which is nothing very much, you just blunder about getting in other people's way and agreeing with anything and everything. And I think I remember the punishment sessions – what the Trank Unit people call Remedials – when they take your mental trousers down and give your mind a good thrashing. I've got scars inside my cheeks. I suppose I must have bitten myself during these sessions. I don't remember any pain, of course. The only painful thing left over from being a Trank are these same scars : nowadays, if I bite carelessly, I nip a sticking-out bit of scar with my molars and that hurts like mad.

I even know what the Remedials were about. I know this not from memory, but by deduction, like Sherlock Holmes. I no longer have much interest in skimmers, so obviously they tranked that part of me. If someone says to me, 'Let's go to the Bevvie Lounge,' I get a sudden wave of panic about the idea of moving from the place where I already am. So obviously they tranked my desire to see new places and things.

They also tranked me on Uncle Lipton. Now, I sweat when he comes anywhere near me. In the old days, I merely wished he'd go away.

But they didn't trank my desire to write. And now, you beautiful, tactful, silent, hidden sheets of paper, I will write down a secret. The secret is this :

I
DANO GAZZARD
OUTRANK
TRANK
!

Just writing it down – scrawling it down in great capitals – inscribing it in beautiful italics – printing it with a curly border round the words – just writing 'I, DANO GAZZARD, OUTRANK TRANK!' gives me the only thrill I ever get in Homebody Unit 362. I love the words. They mean every-thing there is to me. They are my hope, my future, my monument.

And they happen to be true. Yes, I am no longer interested in skimmers. Yes, I am afraid to move from one place to another. Yes, I am physically sickened by Uncle Lipton's presence. Yes, I have been well and truly tranked and it does all sorts of things to me –

But NO, I don't surrender. NO, I won't let my tranking stop me doing what I want to do.

Oh, and a little PS., a little afterthought: guess how many Xtend pills I've got hidden away in a certain place. Ten, do you think? Fifteen? Twenty?

I'll tell you how many I've got.

Enough.

As soon as Uncle Lipton came up to me, I knew that he had been given the same tranking I had received. Even twelve paces away, sweat jumped out on his forehead at the sight of me. Six paces away, he started to cough and choke. The fit was so violent that I thought a vein in his forehead would burst.

Yet he kept coming, staggering and choking across the Bevvie Lounge with the =Gin spilling out of the glass that jiggled in his hand. He kept coming although I had got to my feet and started to back away from him, my heart racing and my mind choking like his throat.

Somehow or other, we managed to stop ourselves from backing away from each other. We overcame the built-in trank waves of repulsion that kept us apart. He managed to choke out, 'Boy! Got to talk to you!' before the coughing started again. Loathing him, I said, 'Yes! Where? When?'

'362-B2,' he gasped, and lurched away. I nodded. 'Twenty minutes,' I said.

Twenty minutes later, I was in 362-B2, the sportsgear store next to our Unit 362, waiting for him. The store room was as good or as bad a place as any other. It wasn't viddied, but Viddy covered the general area of Homebody Unit 362 so someone, presumably, could see Uncle Lipton and I making for our 'secret' meeting place. But then, Viddy monitors are as lazy and inefficient as everyone else. We could be overlooked.

Uncle Lipton came wheezing in, flinching from me at first – just as I did from him – but closing the door and coming towards me all the same. His presence seemed to stifle me. My tranking made me hate every wrinkle on his wrists, every welded seam on his clothing. The mild, familiar smell of =Gin on *his* breath made me feel sick. And he, looking at me, screwed his eyes up with loathing and fear.

'Take my hand, boy,' he said.

I shuddered and drew back. 'You must be mad –'

'Take my hand, Dano. Go on. Shake hands. Take my hand !'

I made myself do it. I took the big, damp, warm, soft hand in my own and held it. I can think of all sorts of disgusting things with which to compare this experience, but I'll spare you them. Enough to say that, tranking or no tranking, we stood there clasping hands.

'Any better?' he said at last. He was trembling and sweating. So was I.

'A bit better,' I lied. 'Keep on . . .'

We stood clasping hands. Eventually he said, 'Right. That's enough. Now wipe your hands, they're sweating filthily –' (he couldn't keep the loathing out of his voice) '– and then stretch out *both* hands, like this, and hold my face.'

Before I could stop him, both hands were on me, grasping my head. I gave some sort of scream and drew away. But he was right, of course : so I moved towards him again, with my own hands outstretched. And soon we were standing there in the gloom, each with our hands on the other's cheeks. If there was a Viddy in the place after all, we must have presented a funny picture.

'Any better?' he asked me again.

'Yes, a bit,' I answered. This time I wasn't lying. It was horrible but bearable.

'I've seen a lot of tranks in my time, boy,' he said. 'Know every tranking trick of the trade. Like eating toads, touching me, isn't it? But you're doing it and you know why you're doing it, right? Right. Then tell me, boy – no, don't move your hands away ! – tell me why we're doing this. For what purpose. Go on, tell me.'

'I can't think properly when I'm touching you, I can't talk –' I said, shivering.

'Oh yes you can !' he said, and lifted one hand long enough to slap my cheek. 'And you *will*,' he said, slapping me again.

'We're doing it,' I began, 'because we've got to get used to each other, in spite of the tranking.'

'Why must we get used to each other, laddie?'

'Because we need each other,' I said.

'Good lad. Why do we need each other?'

'Because we depend on each other,' I answered. I was feeling better by the second. At first, the touch of his hands had been unbearable. Now it was just very unpleasant – like, say, eating something dirty. 'We can't do without each other,' I went on. 'Not if we're ever to be free again. Free to –'

But he covered my mouth with his hand. 'Even the walls have ears, son !' he said, reminding me of the poster with those words on that I used to see in the 1940s. 'We'll go for a slow walk, back to the Bevvie Lounge,' he said, very quietly. 'Can you stand me now?'

'Yes. I'm fine. I don't feel sick any more when you're near me.'

'I feel sick all the time,' he answered. 'But it's nothing to do with you, laddie. It's all *this* that makes me sick ...'

'We've got to get out again, Uncle,' I said. 'Do you think we can go back?'

'Back to where you've been? That farm? And me back to the Officers' Mess? You must be joking !'

'But I didn't do anything wrong, I didn't get into trouble –'

'Makes no difference, son. You've been there once. You can't go back again. You can't stand twice in one pair of shoes.'

'I don't understand you, all I want is to –'

'Think, laddie. Just think for a moment. You went to Halpington Farm, that was the name of the place, wasn't it? You arrived there on a train at such and such a time. You walked over this field or that, stood here, ran there, and so on and so on. So at some time in history, *you were there*. In the flesh. Agreed?'

'Yes, but –'

'So how can you do it again? How can you arrive at Halpington Farm a second time – and find yourself walking towards you? How can you put on your shoes in the morning, and find yourself standing beside yourself trying to put on your shoes?'

He paused, staring at me with his head on one side. I felt he must be right. He sounded so sure of himself.

'There's only room in history, laddie,' he said, 'for *one* guest appearance by you. And even that's chancy enough. But history couldn't stand *two* of you, trying to occupy the same time and space and existence ! Get me?'

I couldn't say anything. I had no answer, only a vision of the blue and white milk jug and an echo of Flo's voice singing a carol in the dairy. I said, 'All right, then. What *can* we do?'

'Can't go back, lad,' said Uncle Lipton, reaching down to whisper in my ear. 'Can't go back – but *can go forward*. Eh? Go forward, eh?'

'No !' I shouted. 'Back ! I want to go back ! You can't stop me ! You're no good without me ! I want to go back !'

'Steady, son, steady!' said Uncle Lipton, staring sideways at me. He was scheming, but I didn't know why or what. His look made me nervous.

'*Can't* we go back, Uncle?' I pleaded.

'Well, you just said I can't stop you, lad. You just told me I'm no good without you. So if you think you can go back – and you won't listen to me –'

'Look, I didn't really mean –'

'I'm sure you didn't, laddie, I'm sure you didn't,' he said, soothingly. But he was still looking sideways at me, working something out. 'I'll tell you what, Dano,' he continued, 'I'll go back with you later if you'll come forward with me first. We *can* go forward, son. It's safe. Eh? What do you say?'

As I was half-silly with my memories of milk jugs and carols, and half-vomiting with the reek of =Gin and frayed nerves, I suppose I can be excused for saying the silliest thing I've ever said.

I said, 'Yes.'

So we trekked forward, into the future. 'Not too far forward,' Uncle Lipton said. 'We just need to find ourselves a convenient hidey-hole in the future, times and places not too foreign to us. Somewhere we could always just slot into when the need arises. Right, boy?'

We found ourselves in surroundings not unlike 2079 and Homebody Unit 362. We were standing in something very like a Bevvie Lounge. The people spoke our language and I immediately recognized the clothing and structural materials – they were much the same as ours.

The big difference was in the way people behaved. Our people, the 2079 people, slouched about : these people moved furtively. Some darted about uneasily, with their eyes flickering from side to side all the time. Others just stood their ground, cautiously looking about, waiting for something to happen. Everyone had a sort of weapon strapped to their waists. You could tell it was a weapon by the way the nervous people kept touching it. There was a notice on the wall saying:

LET'S TALK
NEIGHBOURLY
FIRST!
STUN GUN NO FUN!

Drawings of silly smiling faces surrounded the words. There was an Official Authority code imprint at the bottom of this poster, so obviously it was a properly organized publication, not just a local notice.

Uncle Lipton was already talking to someone, a drab-looking woman who kept smiling. She switched the smile on and off like a flicklight, you could see it was a nervous habit. She said, 'I haven't seen you before, have I? Are you from East Complex?' Uncle Lipton just nodded. She said, 'How are things over there? Bad as – I mean, good as here?' and Uncle Lipton shrugged his shoulders and pulled a face that could have meant anything. Her smile kept coming and going.

Uncle Lipton said, 'Been much trouble, then?' – a clever question because it didn't mean anything until it was answered. The woman answered. Once she started, she just couldn't stop, she put her face right against Uncle Lipton's and mouthed away in his ear. Yet every few seconds, her eyes would flick sideways, searching, and the smile would be switched on again.

'I mean, it's just useless,' she said, tapping the weapon on her hip, 'giving us these things. I mean, a stun wouldn't stop a baby! And *they* come in, and start – well, you know – and if you *use* the stun it's not enough to stop them and if you *don't* use the stun, well it's hopeless, you know – I mean, what are we supposed to do?'

I wanted to know who 'they' were and what 'they' did, but she went rattling on and I couldn't pick up any clues. Then suddenly she stopped and said, her eyes wide, 'You're not carrying a stun! Why ever not? You must be mad, not carrying a stun!'

Uncle Lipton just smiled and nodded over to me. 'I've got *him*,' he said. 'Strong lad. Takes care of himself. And me.'

If I hadn't been so stupid, I would have seen the clues in what Uncle Lipton said. His words proved that he knew what the woman was talking about and that 'they' had to be faced with a stun gun or a 'strong lad'. But I just didn't think.

In fact, I didn't have time to think. There was a roar of skimmers – a great blattering blast as they went over, all of them on plusdrive – and then a dead silence. Everyone in the place just froze in mid-action. Then, slowly, they started murmuring frightened words to each other.

'Perhaps they won't –'

'Perhaps it's not our turn, they were here only last week –'

'It's stupid giving us just these stuns, they're useless –'

'Can't we go back to our units? Perhaps if we hid in our units, they'd –'

'Where are the True Blues, why aren't they coming?'

This last question was answered straight away. The doors burst open and in rushed a crowd of blue-uniformed men, all carrying stuns. They looked pop-eyed with fright. The woman who had been talking to Uncle Lipton said, 'It makes you sick, doesn't it, I mean, they're only allowed stuns, why can't the Official Authority give them proper weapons?' A grey-haired man standing nearby turned round and eyed her sternly, then pointed at a big animated Viddyposter. It was so bright I hadn't even noticed it. It read:

LET'S SETTLE THINGS
THE FRIENDLY WAY

I thought to myself, 'If he's so fond of the poster message, why is his face so white?' I wished I had a stun. I was just about to ask the smiling woman if she'd give me hers when the doors smashed open and I had the answer to my question about who 'they' were.

'They' were boys and girls of my age. There must have

been twenty of them. They all wore ordinary clothes and skimmer gear with one extra item – a pointed hood with two holes cut for the eyes to see through.

They looked very ridiculous and very frightening.

Their leader was a girl. I suppose she must have been about sixteen, I couldn't see her face, but she was big. Her hands had bitten nails and scars along the knuckles. She said, 'Hello and howdy-*doooo*, friends and neighbours! Are we all friends here?'

Nobody said anything. The smiling woman smiled, her lips shaking.

The girl's mocking, little-girl voice continued, 'All friends! Friendly neighbours! Neighbourly friends! Well, that's simply peakview! No need for us!' she said, turning to her gang. 'No work for us here, is there? Because we're the Goodies, aren't we? And we can only do our good deeds where we find Baddies, can't we? And there aren't any Baddies here, are there? Only friends and neighbours. Isn't that right?'

Nobody said anything. The girl took her hood off. She was quite pretty but nasty.

She said, 'Well, that's all rightypighty then! We'll bid you farewellipoos. And goodbyesiwise. We'll be on our merry waysipaisie, that's what we'll be.' She turned to her gang again and asked, 'Don't you so very much agree? You do? Every single one of you? You really do?'

There was silence for a long time. Nothing moved except the smiling woman's lips. Then the gang began taking off their hoods, very deliberately, and one of the gang, a boy older than me and bigger, said, 'I don't agree!' in a harsh voice.

'What, not agree with me? Not agree with Pink Fairy, your leader?' said the girl. You could tell she was loving every minute of it. It was a play she and her gang acted out. My hands were sweating.

'And *why* don't you agree?' the girl said. 'What could

ever be wrong with these lovely dovely friendly neighbours of ours?'

The boy said, 'Stun guns no fun. They got stuns. Not neighbourly.'

'But they're not *carrying* stuns!' said the girl, in her sweet, piping, put-on voice. 'See for yourself, my elf!' She walked up to a man, pulled the stun out of his waist and threw it as hard as she could on to his foot. He yelled and started hopping about.

'There, dear, never fear!' she said. 'He's not carrying a funny stunny, are you, honey?' She walked quickly through the crowd, pulling guns from nerveless fingers and throwing them so that they smashed through windows and Viddy screens, hit people and made them scream.

The True Blues started firing their stuns at the gang. The stuns made a noise like 'chik-ik-ik!' People hit by the beams staggered and toppled, faces writhing, but they didn't go down. Certainly they weren't stunned. Several of the gang were hit, but it made no difference – they just waded in, using their hands likes blades, cutting and chopping at the people. They chanted, 'STUN GUN NO FUN!' louder and louder, all the time.

There were people lying on the floor groaning – people knotted in a corner, their arms clasped over their heads – people bleeding. The True Blues got the worst of it. Two or three gang members would attack one True Blue and chop at him till he went down. I kept backing away, backing away ... my head was clear enough to lead me to safety, but I was terrified.

And then the girl was standing on a table, shouting, 'Stop! Stopitty-poppity! Enoughypuffy!' in her horrible mocking little-girl voice, and everything stopped. I had time to see that the smiling woman, unhurt, was still smiling in a ghastly way – and that Uncle Lipton's face was blotched with white and purple and sweat (but he had found a safe place behind a counter) – that one woman, grey-green in the face, lay on the floor with the whites of her eyes showing – I had time to see all this before I saw that the girl on the table was staring at *me*.

'You're new!' she cried, letting her voice rise to a squeak of little-girl pleasure. She jumped off the table and strode over to me. 'A new friend! A new neighbour!' She patted my face. 'Where are you from, you lovely boy?'

I said nothing.

'East?' she said. 'You're from the East Complex?' I said nothing and she suddenly twisted my nose, very hard, with two fingers. Tears spurted out of my eyes. I knew what a fool I looked.

'They're ever so good and true in the East,' she said. 'They really do believe everything our weedy leaders tell them. Now, this lovely laddie,' she continued, 'was being a very good boy. He wasn't even carrying a stun, were you?' She twisted my nose again. 'Were you, were you, *were you?*'

I couldn't see her for the tears.

'Such a *good* boy,' she said in her baby voice. 'Like us. W*e* don't carry stuns. W*e* don't use weapons. Not ever, ever, ever! We just go chippitty-choppitty, chippitty-choppitty –'

She was hitting me with her hands, then her fists, as hard as she could. Even as she hit me, I remembered fighting a boy who lived in a cottage near Halpington Farm. We used to fight for fun, but we fought harder and harder as the weeks went by until we were permanently covered with bruises and cuts. I was thinking of this boy while she hit me – thinking that though she was a big girl and was doing her worst, she still couldn't punch nearly as hard as that boy near Halpington Farm.

Then Uncle Lipton shouted, 'Belt her one, boy!' and without thinking, I did. I felt my fist crack against her cheekbone and heard her fall over. I wiped my eyes quickly to clear the tears just in time to see a boy from the gang coming towards me, fists raised. I let him come just the right distance and then punched. His head seemed to bounce away from my fist and I felt the shock go right through my arm and down through my body to the floor. It was a glorious feeling.

But then they were all on me, all hitting me, and I didn't know what to do any more. I tried to curl up into a ball to keep my head covered. They went on and on hitting me until the girl stopped them.

She dropped her little-girl voice and spoke in her own harsh, coarse voice. 'Leave him alone,' she said. 'Stop it.' They stopped. She knelt beside me and said, 'We're going to smear you. You're going to be smeared all over this region. Do you understand?'

I got to my feet slowly, trying to think of something to say – and hoping that Uncle Lipton would help me. I muttered something about not understanding.

She said, 'You – are – going – to – be – smeared. We're going to drag you hanging from a skimmer at roof height until there's nothing left to drag except the rope. Understand that?'

'You can't do that, you'll get caught and punished –'

She laughed. 'Who'll catch us? Who'll punish us? The Official Authority?' She went on laughing in a forced sort of way and some of her gang joined in.

The smiling woman suddenly burst out with a stream of words about wickedness, how justice would catch up with them one day and why couldn't they leave decent people alone; but she soon quietened down and just sobbed. However, she said enough to prove how hopeless my position was. In 2079, the Official Authority had power; if you were naughty you were more or less spanked, and if you were very naughty you were tranked. But in this future time, Official Authority had no power. Nobody could save me, unless –

I looked for Uncle Lipton and found him. Our eyes met. His face was no longer patchy and frightened. It was almost sneering.

'They're going to kill you, laddie,' he said. 'This is 2084 and they're going to kill you. You die in 2084, right?'

I couldn't understand him and said, 'But Uncle Lipton –'

'2079 to 2084,' he said. 'That's five years. Five years precisely.'

I still couldn't understand what he was getting at. No one
else could either. Everything had stopped while he spoke.
Nobody did anything.

'But aren't you even going to try and save me –' I began.

'Save you?' he said. 'From this shower? Too easy, lad ! Of
course I can save you ! You want to be saved? You are asking
me to save you?'

'Yes, of course, I don't understand . . .'

He came over to me with his hand outstretched. The girl
and the gang did not try to stop him. They were as mystified
as I was.

'Just take my hand, laddie,' said Uncle Lipton. 'Take my
hand and we'll go on a trek. I've been in the travelling game
longer than you, you know. All sorts of tricks up my
sleeve . . .'

While he spoke, the room seemed to shift and twist. I saw
the gang girl coming towards me, her clenched fist stuck out
and her mouth and eyes angry and open. I saw members of
the gang running towards me. But even as I looked at them,
I experienced the queasy, sick, lurching sensation I half remembered before, at Claypole's Pond near Halpington
Farm –

The sensation sharpened as if my insides were being sucked
out of me –

'Now, laddie,' said Uncle Lipton, comfortably, 'I want you
to drink up your NuChoc and listen very carefully to what
your dear old Nunky has to say. Are you listening?'

We were back in 2079.

He explained. He explained very clearly. He made it quite
plain what a fool I had allowed him to make of me and what
a hopeless position I was now in.

'Five years, laddie,' he said, smiling and sneering. 'That's your life expectation as from this moment. You have five years to live. Simple mathematics. Subtract 2079 from 2084 – you get five.'

'And in 2084, I get smeared – killed?' I said.

'Yes, boy o' mine,' he said cheerfully. 'You get killed absolutely dead. And very painfully. Unless –'

'Unless what?'

'Unless you are a particularly good and obedient little lad and do exactly what your dear old Uncle tells you to do,' he said. 'Then you don't get killed at all. You live out your natural life. No smearing, no mob of nasty yobbos waiting to flay you alive – just a jolly, happy, ordinary little life. A quiet grave and a hallowed tomb, all that sort of thing. Either that – or five years and *whoompf*! By which I mean, *smear*!'

'You keep saying five years. How do I know it's five years? I didn't see a calendar, it could have been any time. It needn't even have been 2084 –'

'Clever lad,' said Uncle Lipton approvingly. 'Now tell me I'm a liar about the *place*, as well as the time.'

'I'm not calling you a liar about the place,' I said. 'It happened in a Bevvie Lounge all right. Just like ours.'

'Which proves, does it not, that you can expect something nasty to happen in a place very like this, at some future time rather like our time?'

'Yes. I admit that.'

'And you admit that the sort of yobbos who threatened to smear you are the sort of people our society is producing right now?'

'Yes. They'd even got skimmers. But how do I know you weren't lying about the date? My smearing might never take place at all if that gang of yobbos were a long time ahead in the future. Not five years, but – well, say, seventy.'

I thought about what I had been saying. It made some sense, but not a lot. So it was almost an appeal when I asked Uncle Lipton, 'W*ere* you lying about 2084?'

'Who knows, laddie, who knows?' he said, and roared with

laughter. 'You don't know, do you? And if I know, do you think I'll tell? No, laddie, only one thing is absolutely certain as far as you're concerned: there's something nasty waiting for you in the nearish future. Death, laddie, violent death, in any of the next few years. You've seen the people who are going to kill you. You can't avoid them. They're waiting for you.'

'I *can* avoid them,' I said. 'Now I know about them, I'll just keep clear of that situation. I mean, when I see that bit of history coming up – those gang people in their skimmers and everything – I'll just keep out of the way.'

'No, laddie, not so,' he chuckled. 'No escape. For one thing, your memory won't last that long. Things will fade, you know they will. You've got to live in a continuing present – live *now* – and that wipes memories out. I know, laddie, I know. I've done it all so often. The old fog thickens and blurs the mind . . . it's happened to me again and again –'

'I can write it down,' I said.

'Keep a diary of the future, you mean? When you don't know any exact dates and times? Oh, you're a great scribbler, boy. I know all about that. But you'll find this piece of writing a little difficult. Wouldn't bother if I were you . . .'

He got himself another =Gin, smiling at people around him at the bar. He came back and settled himself into his chair again.

'Well, lad?' he said, cocking his head confidently. 'Well?'

In the minute or so he had been away, I had been trying to test what he had told me. I cast my mind back to Halpington Farm. Surely I could remember everything clearly? Surely the memories couldn't fade?

And suddenly I couldn't remember the colour of the panel in the front of the piano. I could see the gingery wood all right – all the panels framing the centre panel. But this centre panel I could no longer *see*. I *knew* what it looked like, it had flowers writhing about. But I couldn't *see* it any more in my mind.

'Here's health, laddie!' said Uncle Lipton, raising his glass. 'And I really do mean that. Health, lad! Continuing health! A long life and a happy one!'

I felt sick and tired and empty. 'All right, then,' I said, 'how do I stay healthy? What do I have to do?'

'Whatever I want you to do, lad,' he said. 'Now, I'll be quite frank with you. Tell you everything. First, I'm getting on a bit. Must happen, no arguing with it – after all, I'm the longest-lived man in the history of the world!

'Second, I'm losing a bit of my grasp where Xtend is concerned. Seem to need more and more of the stuff and even then I can't be sure of results. They won't give me enough Xtend, I've tried it on. And even if they did, I'm not sure I could make use of it.

'Third, there's you. Now, I never told you this (of course I didn't, I'm not a fool) but as soon as you took Xtend – as soon as we, so to speak, joined hands and cooperated in taking Xtend – I found it suddenly easier to get things right and take off in time. You were a godsend, laddie. You gave me back my old power. Without you, I don't think I'd be able to time-travel. I mean, your young, strong mind, your will, your newness –'

He went maundering on, his eyes damp with goodwill towards me, until I interrupted. 'You tell me all this,' I said, 'and in the same breath tell me that you've lined me up for a horrible death – smeared by that gang and their skimmers –'

'Quite so, laddie!' he said cheerfully. 'Mustn't get carried away, must I? Very grateful to you for your youth, and innocence and so on, but business first.'

'What business?' I replied wearily.

'Doing whatever I want to do, laddie. Going wherever I want to go. Using *you*, laddie, to get me away from this hideous, mediocre time and place, into the wild blue yonder!'

'So I'm to be your slave?' I said.

'That's it, laddie, that's it precisely!' he roared. 'Glad you cottoned on so quickly. Slave, that's the word. Take the pills when I tell you. Help me get away when I want to get away. Save me from making a fool of myself – I admit it, oh yes, I admit I can be naughty sometimes – when we're away from now and somewhere out there. Do exactly what I tell you, when I tell you, and double-quick about it. A slave !'

'And if I agree, I don't get killed in 2084 or whenever it is?'

'Quite so. You don't get killed in 2084 *or whenever it is.* Sly dog, aren't I? Mind you, you'll have fun too. We'll have great times together. And I promise you faithfully that we won't go anywhere near that frightful time and place with that awful girl and her skimmer gang. Nothing for you to fear at all.'

'How can I rely on you?'

'What, to keep my word? You can't rely on my word, sonny Jim. All you can rely on is this : if you do exactly what I tell you to do, you *very probably* have some sort of a life ahead of you. But if you don't do what you're told, you'll *quite certainly* come to a sticky end. Satisfied?'

'Yes,' I said. 'Quite satisfied. Completely satisfied.' I left him smiling to himself, drinking =Gin, and went to bed. I didn't even cry myself to sleep, or anything dramatic like that. I just lay in the dark, staring at nothing. Numb.

And then I started thinking. I thought until I'd pinned it down – Uncle Lipton's big lie.

The big lie was this : when I told him that I wanted to go back to the Halpington Farm days, he had said, 'You've been there once. You can't go back again. You can't stand twice in the same pair of shoes. If you went back to Halpington Farm, you might meet yourself coming round a corner.'

You remember that? You do? Good. I remembered it and assumed it to be true. Or perhaps I was just puzzled. I never thought his argument through.

But then, remembering the girl and the skimmer gang and the beating-up in the Bevvie Lounge, I realized that Uncle Lipton must have been giving me a false argument about going back to Halpington Farm. He had told me the big lie. Because, you see, *he himself had been in that Bevvie Lounge before*. Or so he claimed. He knew what was going to happen, knew the gang was coming, knew that my life would be threatened at that particular time in that particular place. Or so he said.

So what was to stop me from going back to Halpington Farm, on my own? If Uncle Lipton could revisit the past, why not I? Why not escape to the time when I was happy?

There were several reasons why. Uncle Lipton was the boss. He was in control because he was the adult and I was the boy. So if he said 'You, boy! Come with me!' I'd have to go. And if he got himself into serious trouble, I would have to go with him when the fuss started.

Still more important was the 'Time to go' feeling. Uncle Lipton had warned me of it and I had experienced it. I knew the Feeling could and did happen. Something told me that if I returned to Halpington Farm, the Feeling would strike at me very soon. I'd already had my time there.

Was Uncle Lipton lying when he said I would be killed by the Pink Fairy and her gang if I didn't obey him? Could he arrange for me to go back to *exactly* the same time and place? I think he was lying, because so many things about Pink Fairy and her gang could change between the first and second visits. When you time-trek, you travel in your own person, your own age. True, Uncle Lipton first time-trekked as a toddler (that was when he picked up the ration books). But on that trek, he wasn't in control. He was having an unexpected dream that 'came true'. When you consciously and deliberately make a time-trek happen, you're not dreaming. You're *you*.

What does happen when you time-trek?

I think it is this: you slip yourself on to another time track. You shift from your mainline rails on to any one of an infinite number of other rails, running parallel. Uncle Lipton's mind might lead him and me to Pink Fairy: your mind might lead you to a polar ice cap and a big white bear. In 2084 I found myself in a life-or-death situation: you might find yourself in a 2084 hot bath. It all depends where you start from, which is another way of saying *who you are*.

Anyhow, that's what I believe (I think). And it seems to fit in with what happened to Uncle Lipton and me (I think).

But perhaps I haven't thought long enough or well enough.

Perhaps nobody can.

One thing was certain. Now I was Uncle Lipton's slave, I might as well enjoy myself. So we trekked and travelled as much as our supplies of Xtend (and the Official Authority) would let us.

I still don't know what the Official Authority thought of our appearances and disappearances. I suppose that, because of Uncle Lipton's status as freak and nonconformist, they just let him do as he pleased. They gave him up, and me with him.

Or perhaps it was that they had more serious things to think about. Two things were happening at the same time in 2079.

First, the kids in their skimmers were becoming far too important: they were beginning to dominate and destroy the Official Authority's society. The breed of Pink Fairy yobbos who beat me up were already beginning to take over. The whole idea behind life and society in 2079 was *Conform – be like the others – drink your Bevvie and shut up*. The kids in their skimmers wouldn't conform and wouldn't shut up. They wanted fun and excitement – even danger.

The second thing on the Official Authority's mind was Reclamation. You know all about this, of course, they were always talking about Reclamation on the Viddy. But they don't tell you the truth. They don't dare. The truth is (and I know what I'm talking about, because I've travelled into the future) that Reclamation actually *works*. The forbidden lands, the wastelands burned and poisoned in the third world war (remember me telling you that London was a desert?) were beginning to be reclaimed. There were hints that people might once again live in the forbidden territories and in the open air.

Now, as I say, they were always talking about Reclamation on the Viddy. And then – did you notice? – they stopped talking about it. There were no more programmes about the Wonder Workers of the Wastelands, etc. Why? Because the Official Authority very soon realized that they should never have raised the subject in the first place: it made people discontented. Discontented with their shabby, cramped, crowded, mean little lives. Discontented with living like battery hens. Discontented with the whole business of being half-alive in 2079.

So the programmes on the Viddy stopped, but the Reclamation work went on. Even in your very own Homebody Unit, you must have heard rumours about a kid who took his skimmer, went natural – and survived. Perhaps you've even met a Teen who claims to have lived Out There for weeks on end. You've wondered about the different look in his eyes and thought to yourself, 'Is he just a psycho who likes telling lies – or has he really seen something I've never seen?'

My answer to that question is, 'Yes, he's seen something. He really has. He's seen something bigger than a Homebody Unit and he can't get it out of his mind!'

And I can tell you what he's seen. Because I've seen it too.

In fact, the very next trip Uncle Lipton made me take was to the future. I say 'made me take', but of course I was willing to go. I just wished that I could go on my own.

We travelled forward about 150 years – I can't be sure just how far – and found ourselves in a field with small grey houses every half mile or so.

We knew it was a field because there were vegetables

growing and the area was edged with concrete fences, like all the other fields. We didn't know, however, what year we were in, or even what century. There were no people in sight to tell us.

We began walking to the nearest grey house. When we got near the house, a trap door opened in the side and a hooter began to make a regular wailing noise. Then, from the trap door, a machine about the size of a dog came out. It wobbled along on its air cushion, going surprisingly fast and squirting violet liquid from what must have been a series of nozzles inside its casing. It came straight towards us, looking a bit silly but very determined. We ran away. It chased us.

Then Uncle Lipton tripped and fell – I stopped to help him – and the machine gave us a good sprinkling of its violet liquid.

I still have faint violet patches on the back of my neck and right hand and Uncle Lipton's right leg was violet to the knee for a long time – he had kicked the machine over on its side and his leg got a thorough soaking.

When we got back to 2079 – and we got back as quick as we could – and when Uncle Lipton had quite finished swearing, he said, 'Well, at least it's not poison.'

'What's not poison?'

'The violet stuff. It couldn't be.'

'Why not? Obviously that machine was a sort of watchdog, so –'

'Stands to reason. It was protecting crops – stuff to be eaten. So they wouldn't run the risk of using a poison. That liquid was just a dye. Anyone comes trespassing and they get dyed a nasty colour. Very sensible idea. Makes identification easy.'

'It was a very big, wide place, wasn't it, Uncle?'

'There you are, then. We've learned something. Reclamation actually works. There were fields as far as the eye could see. But the ground was quite flat. So almost certainly that was reclaimed land.'

'It's no good, however much you rub, the violet won't come off,' I said.

That evening, Uncle Lipton tried rubbing his stains with =Gin. Funnily enough, it was the only thing that did any good.

It was on the next trip, perhaps 200 years ahead, that we first met and got to know humans of the future. They called themselves Aristos. They lived in a reclaimed town in what Uncle Lipton thinks was the country once called France. They can't have been 'typical' people of their period, just a gang of isolated madmen.

'Our welcome most profound,' said their spokesman, 'to the kingdom of the Aristos!' He made a sort of bow. His clothes were grand in a filthy, smelly sort of way – a great sweeping cloak of rotting velvet with gold tassels, knee boots cut from the sort of plastic wall covering you see in Bevvie Lounges and a ridiculous hat like a turban with a great red jewel in it.

I did not know how to reply to this person, and waited for Uncle Lipton to say something. But he was making choking noises and turning brick red. Later, he told me why: he had recognized the jewel in the turban as a red reflector from the mudguard of an old, twentieth-century bicycle! Uncle Lipton was trying not to laugh.

At last Uncle Lipton managed to say, 'Jolly decent of you, I'm sure. Most welcome, this – welcome of yours. The kingdom of Aristos, you say? Who's the king?'

'I am,' said the spokesman, making great play with his cloak and showering bits of gold tassel everywhere.

He conducted us round his kingdom, which consisted of some thirty houses and his own 'palace' – a larger house. Once, obviously, the kingdom had been a rural village. Now it was a kingdom whose true king was nostalgia for the past. 'The golden lustre of the long-ago . . . the hallowed memories of the – ah! but I see you are observing my portraits. Let me conduct you through the gallery myself . . .'

He took us through his portrait gallery. There were pictures and busts of Nero, the Lone Ranger, Little Nell, the Beatles, Florence Nightingale – almost anyone you care to mention (Uncle Lipton told me later that the King had got most of the names wrong). I wasn't thinking about the King's portraits. I was thinking about his kingdom. I looked out of the windows, over the rolling fields. Huge fields, each a different colour. How different from the Homebody Units of 2079 !

'One of my ancestors,' announced the King, flicking a dirty ruffled wrist at a plaster bust of Beethoven. Uncle Lipton made a small bow at the little statue. His neck was swelling with laughter again. But I was looking for houses among the fields and landscapes. Sometimes I could pick out what could have been a real home. Or was it just a pumping station or the dwelling unit of a guardian robot?

Later, we had dinner. I could make you laugh about that dinner – about the King passing round a 'bumper' of =Gin, with fruit juice in it, as if it were some sort of rare vintage wine; about the awful food in the beautiful real china plates (but some lesser Lords and Barons had to eat off Klenzware, just like the people in 2079). I could make you laugh, as I say, but I found it all a bit sad and boring. And anyhow, it didn't matter. What mattered was, as Uncle Lipton said that night when we were shown to our grand, lofty, smelly, dirty, bedroom –

'So there is a future after all, lad. Something bigger and better than 2079, wouldn't you agree?'

'I suppose so. But these old lunatics, they're not exactly better than the 2079 people –'

'You're missing the point, laddie, as usual. Someone cooked that ghastly food. Someone put it on plates. Someone grew it, collected it, delivered it. Some society exists which tolerates and contributes to the existence of the crazy King and his crazy Aristos. Get my point?'

'Reclamation ... all it leads to is this stupid gang of Aristos !' I said. 'Looking at them, you begin to wonder whether it wasn't better in the days of the Official Authority !'

And suddenly Uncle Lipton was in a towering rage with me. He jumped up off the edge of his bed and stood over me, shouting and lecturing me about the Dignity of Man, and Freedom of Choice and the Tyranny of Sameness. I couldn't understand why he was so worked up about defending the Aristos.

When he ran out of breath for a moment, I said, 'If the Aristos represent the Dignity of Man, I can do without –'

But he would not let me finish. He said the Aristos were free men, they did not conform, they were dignified and 'heroic'.

'As if the Aristos mattered !' I said, angrily. 'Now, if you were talking about the Halpington Farm people –'

'Don't you see, laddie,' he interrupted, 'it's all the same thing !'

'No, I don't see !' I replied and turned over in bed with my back to him. 'Anyway,' I said, turning over again to accuse him, 'you're a fine one to talk ! You, talking about heroes ! You, telling me about the dignity of man ! You of all people !'

And I rolled over yet again, pulled the musty bedclothes over my noble head and went to sleep.

You see, I simply couldn't understand what he meant. How could I have understood, then?

And how can I forgive myself, now that it's too late?

Heroes. Greatness. The dignity of the human spirit ...

The only heroes and great men I wanted to see belonged to the known past, not to the unknown future. The past has happened. The future has not. So when we left the Aristos (which we did at dawn, the night after our quarrel, without saying goodbye), I said, 'Uncle, if we're on speaking terms, I'd like to talk about our next trip.'

He said, 'Keep your voice down, boy.' We were back in

2079, sitting in the Bevvie Lounge. He looked around and said, 'All right. Go on. Next trip to where?'

'The past, Uncle. You talk about heroes. Well, I've got heroes of my own and I want to see them. But they're all in the past.'

To my surprise, he agreed straight away. He seemed to have forgotten our quarrel. 'The past it is, lad!' he said. 'Anyhow, it's easier going back than forward.'

I went to get him a drink. When I came back with it, he had thought my suggestion over and worked himself up into one of his enthusiasms. 'Dickens, lad!' he boomed, not caring who overheard. 'The real England! Dingley Dell and Fagin's den and the Dover Road and Mr Bumble the Beadle! Chop houses and coaching inns! That's the time and place for us, lad! The happy and glorious reign of Queen Victoria!'

Well, that's what Uncle Lipton said. What we found was something quite different. We emerged in a little shop in Holloway – it seemed Uncle Lipton was managing it while the owner ('Geo. Metternich, Confectioner') was away on some business or other. The shop was miserable, yet we seldom left it: perhaps it was Uncle Lipton's spiritual home. It sold confectionery – licorice straps with a coloured sugar bead in the middle, a sickening 'sucker' sweet called Egg and Bacon, gobstoppers, sherbert fountains, a toffee called Jaw-breaker and a glassy sort that had to be shattered with a little brass hammer.

But confectionery was only part of the business. We also stocked colza oil for oil lamps (I can smell it still, the stink even got into the sweet jars), black lead for the servants to black grates with, hearthstone powder for them to whiten front door steps, knife powder to clean cutlery, mousetraps, galvanized pails, hide food for cleaning leather, stale cheese, lamp wicks – all sorts of basic necessities. Everything seemed to cost halfpennies and farthings and was dear at the price. However, we charged nothing for the mouse droppings in the flour barrel or the rat bites in the cheese – or the smell of colza that we served with everything.

My job, among others, was to be delivery boy. We had two sorts of customers: those who came into the shop and carried their purchases away, and those who had the goods delivered by me, to the back door through the Tradesmen's Entrance.

The cash-and-carry customers were skivvies, the lowest among the servant girls; or filthy children, wasting their farthings and halfpennies on the rotten sweets we sold; or filthy old men and women who needed two candles, or 'a little cheese for the mousetrap' (poor wretches, we knew and they knew that they'd eat the mouldy, cracked, rock-hard cheese themselves).

The smell of the colza oil was like violets after the smell of some of our customers. I used to keep my eyes off their noses – particularly the children's: there must have been something about the mixture of sooty yellow air, rising damp, fog, smoke, gas fumes, stopped drains and crumbling brickwork that gave everyone an everlastingly running nose.

Sometimes we'd get women shuffling into the shop carrying bundles. 'It's Mr Metternich I want,' they'd say, looking about anxiously.

'Away on business, my good woman,' replied Uncle Lipton (he soon got into the way of calling people 'My good woman', 'My good man' and 'young feller me lad').

'When'll 'e be back, for Gawd's sake?'

'No saying, my good woman.'

So the 'good woman' would curse, or snivel, or argue, according to her nature, and go away with her bundle. Uncle Lipton would prod the air three separate times with his forefinger, making a triangular pattern, and sing, 'Bing ... bang ... bong!' and nod, and look very wise.

He explained to me what this pantomime meant. The shop was only a front for Mr Metternich's real trade, which was that of unlicensed pawnbroker. Proper pawnbrokers' shops had a trademark: three brass balls arranged in a triangle. Bing, bang, bong.

'Astute gentleman, our Mr Metternich,' said Uncle Lipton. 'First, he robs the poor by taking any money they possess in exchange for bad goods. Then he robs them again by taking the money they haven't even got yet!'

'What do you mean, Uncle?'

'Pawnbroking, laddie. If you put something into pawn, the broker lends you some small part of its value. Take that woman who came in just now. I don't know what she had in that bundle, it could have been anything from her husband's working tools to her own bedding ... Well, old Metternich would advance her a few pennies for whatever it was, and hang on to the goods. When the woman wants them back, she gives our Mr M. the pennies back – plus a few more. Quite a few more ... and so our Mr M. gets rich.'

'Suppose she never can afford to buy her things back?'

'Then Mastermind Metternich flogs them and keeps the money. Heads he wins, tails you lose.'

'I don't see what you're laughing at. I don't think it's at all funny.'

'It's appalling, lad!' beamed Uncle Lipton. 'It's unjust! It's tragic! That's the joke!'

I looked around the hideous little shop, lit only by the nasty, uncertain light of two fishtail gas burners. In one corner, blocking a mousehole, there was my delivery basket, filled with orders for me to deliver. I looked down at my own feet, with their clumsy lace-up boots. Then I looked at Uncle Lipton. He was pouring himself a third of a tumbler of gin from a dark bottle. Gin was the cheapest thing you could buy. Uncle Lipton never stopped buying it and pouring it down his throat. It made his face thick and dull red.

'I've got another good joke for you, Uncle,' I said. 'We're leaving. Now. Immediately.'

'We can't do that, lad!' said Uncle Lipton, open-mouthed.

'Mr Metternich isn't back yet! We can't just close down the shop! *It wouldn't be honest!*'

The weird thing about Uncle Lipton is, that he really meant it.

We got back to 2079 and the Homebody Unit and the Viddy, the Viddy, the everlasting Viddy.

That night there was 3-wall VividViddy. The Bevvie Lounge was flooded with Viddy. The Official Authority was bombing our minds with a new GLORIOUS HERITAGE! peakview feature. I think they put out these peakviews to stop us hankering after the wide-open spaces promised by Reclamation some time in the future; and to stop us hankering after the wide-open spaces known to everyone in the past. After all, the glorious past contained an awful lot of human misery and demanded the sort of toughness that no 2079 person could stand for three minutes. So the Official Authority won both ways – and we homebodies were made to feel nice and cosy about living in the present, yet somehow noble in our niceness and cosiness.

I didn't pay full attention to the programme. Or I tried not to. The past I knew wasn't much like the Glorious Past being shown on the three walls of the Bevvie Lounge. But I couldn't escape the plugs, nobody could. How *can* you escape when the best brains and techniques of 2079 are trying to sell you something? You just can't switch yourself off when all three walls are glowing with colours, pulsing with sounds and shapes, jetting fragrances. And of course you're actually made to *feel*, with your hands or mouth or whole body, the newest This-You-Must-Have peakview purchase.

I remember they plugged the Skarlet Starlet, the skimmer with Plusdrive Plus. I tried not to tune to it, but what can you do when you find yourself swept along with a blattering, howling roar, and you feel the control bar in one hand and the Plusdrive Plus knob in the other – and the voice is saying, right inside your head, 'Fantass, feller! ... Set her screaming! ... Let her leap! ... Cut in that plus-plus and – YEOW! – let's GO!' They'd even got that hot electrical smell right. You just can't avoid tuning, the Viddy is too strong to resist.

But I resisted without much effort when the Vitalacto plug came on. Vitalacto is that dingy synthetic milk, nobody but the Official Authority likes it (and they must like it a lot, or have too much of it – it's always being plugged). Anyhow, there was the Viddy making you 'run the silky green grass through your hands ... because, yes-oh-yes folks, Vitalacto is made Dame Nature's very own way, from tender green grasses reared by loving hands in the gardens of Hydroponia ...'

And all of a sudden I didn't feel those 'loving hands' stroking my cheeks. I didn't smell or feel the 'silky green grass' brushing my palms. I saw and felt and smelled Halpington Farm.

'Halpington Farm!' I said, out loud. Uncle Lipton heard me. 'You and your damned farm!' he grumbled.

'What do you mean? What's wrong with Halpington Farm?' I said. It was safe to talk, the Viddy had everyone else trapped.

'Same thing as was wrong with Metternich's establishment, laddie!' he said. 'Both of them out of date. Old hat. Rotten.'

'Halpington Farm wasn't rotten, it was –'

'End of an era, laddie. Last wriggle of the nineteenth century's tail. Feudalistic nonsense. Pipe-dream.'

'Well, I like that! After all the things you've said ...! And you seemed happy enough –'

'Me, lad? Why talk about me? I'm just a has-been, like Halpington Farm. A relic of the old days.'

I didn't know what to say to this. You never know what to say when people speak your own unkind thoughts about them.

Uncle Lipton said, fiercely, 'You're young, lad! Young, young, young! You should be looking to the future – building the future!'

'Like you, Uncle?' I said, sneeringly. I wanted to hurt him.

'No, laddie, not like me,' he said. 'Don't do what I do. Do what I *did*. Look!'

And there on the Viddy – but only on two walls – they were showing the galactic shot: Uncle Lipton's spaceshot! I saw spacemen (was one of them Uncle Lipton?) settling down at old-fashioned controls, or climbing through hatches, or staring into the sky and looking noble. I glanced sideways at Uncle Lipton. His face was set and his mouth pursed. A pulse in the side of his neck was beating fast, jumping under the skin.

'Flinging their challenge to the very stars!' boomed the voice-over. It was a meaty, Official Authority voice. 'Adventuring fearlessly to the limits of space! Thrusting outwards and onwards –'

Suddenly, sickeningly, it was a joke. Yes, a joke. They'd speeded up the projection of the old film so that people moved jerkily, jumpily, like cartoon characters. Silver-clad, space-helmeted figures nodded and jabbered and waddled. Legs moved grotesquely fast. Toy-like vehicles mickeymoused across tarmac lined with crowds who whinnied 'Hurray!' in tinny treble voices.

People in the Bevvie Lounge began to laugh. The laughter took hold and became a roar when the Viddy people pulled an even funnier trick. 'Blast off!' cried the meaty voice-over, and the ship lifted a little from its clouds of smoke and steam: but then the clever Viddy people had looped the film so that you saw the same sequence repeated over and over again – the ship lifting then settling back, lifting and settling. And all the time the voice-over shouted, 'Blast off! I said, *Blast off!* No, seriously now, fellers, BLAST OFF! ... Well, now, folks, seems like there's a little trouble there, heh-heh! Seems like that old sky-sausage just don't *want* to blast off ...'

I looked at Uncle Lipton: and looked away very quickly. I can still see his face as it was in that split second.

Later I found courage to speak to him. I didn't say the things I wanted to say. I just said, 'Shall we go on a trek, Uncle?' He nodded, heavily. 'Yes. Trek.' He spoke as if his tongue was swollen. I said, 'Good. We'll do it soon,' and walked away.

He called after me, 'You're a good lad, Dano,' and I choked and started running.

We went to the future. By now, I seemed to be setting the pace for our trips more than Uncle Lipton. 'Anywhere but here, laddie,' he used to say. 'Any time but now. I leave it to you.'

So I craftily planned future trips, thinking that the more I knew about the future, the better. Uncle Lipton had threatened me with the future and I wanted to meet his threat with at least some knowledge of what I had to face.

But of course, all the time my heart was in Halpington Farm. It was there that I wanted to be. That was the place to which I would escape some bright and beautiful day – *if*. There were so many *ifs*. If Uncle Lipton had lied when he told me that one could never visit the same place twice – and *if* his lies had been complete lies, not just half-in-half lies – and *if* I could only settle in the past, without those awful sudden flashes from the future, the warning voices saying, 'You must come back!' If only I could work out the real truth about some or all of these *ifs*, then just possibly I could escape Uncle Lipton, the future, the present and the threat to my own life.

By chance, we hit on very nearly the identical place where we had met the Stun Guns and the True Blues and the skimmer gang with the girl leader. Obviously it was not the same Homebody Unit, nor was the time precisely the same. But somehow it all felt the same. There was the same sterile nastiness, the same metallic threat, in the air. The people looked the same and glanced about them nervously in the same way, waiting for trouble. The Homebody Unit and the Bevvie Lounge were just the same, but of course they are the same everywhere.

I said conversationally, '2084, Uncle? Or thereabouts, wouldn't you say?'

He just mumbled something and stared uneasily at nothing in particular.

'Good time and place for me to meet my death,' I said. He didn't seem to hear. 'Just the right place to get smeared,' I went on. 'Just the right atmosphere. I get killed in 2084 or thereabouts, don't I? Unless I obey you? Well, wouldn't you describe this as 2084 or thereabouts?'

He wasn't listening to me. His eyes were vaguely scanning the tops of the buildings and the sky beyond. I thought, 'You're getting old, Uncle Lipton. In spite of Xtend.' And it was true that the old boy did suddenly seem to have added another fifteen years to his age. He was slowing down, getting pouchier, losing interest. He had got into the habit of letting me take care of our trips. It was my will, my mental energy, that launched us.

'Don't like this place, laddie,' he said, out of the blue. 'Damn dull. Damn threatening. Damn ugly.'

'Good place for me to die,' I said, trying again to rouse him so that I could learn something from him. Had he planned it all? Was he going to kill me here?

But he wasn't listening. He was sniffing at the sky again. 'Die when I want you to,' he muttered absent-mindedly. 'Don't want you dead yet.'

'What do you want, Uncle?' I said. 'A drink? I'll bet it's a drink you want.'

'There's skimmers somewhere around,' he mumbled, 'somewhere close. I could swear to it. Trouble on the way, laddie . . .'

I too began 'sniffing' at the sky. I knew at once that he was right. Suddenly there seemed to be no people in sight.

Doors and windows were closed. You could see nothing fearful, yet could feel fear.

'Let's get out of this ghastly –' Uncle Lipton began, when a pulse of air reached us – then a howl of sound – and the skimmers came.

The wingtip of the very first of the skimmers hit Uncle Lipton's left shoulder. The blow threw him twenty feet, slam against the wall of a Bevvie Lounge. When he got up, there was a wet red patch on the wall and his arm dangled. Blood dripped down his hand. His mouth opened and closed. His face was patchy with cold sweat and shock.

I yelled something to him, but of course he could not hear, the skimmers were whistling and screeching across and across, cutting in their plusdrives at the bottom of the dive. I pulled at Uncle Lipton's good arm and somehow got him to the door of the Bevvie Lounge. The door opened, but only an inch : someone on the other side was keeping it shut. I yelled, 'Man hurt ! Let me in !' but a pale face, with more pale faces behind, shouted something that meant, 'No !'

A skimmer took the Viddy tower off the top of the building. The skimmer's wing simply sliced right through the tower. I remember thinking, as the tower exploded into bits and pieces of electronic equipment and aerial and plastic Brix, 'That's one of the skimmers gone !' – but I was wrong, I saw the same skimmer (it had a violet colorflux finish, like powdered metal with lights behind it) come over and knock the tower off another Bevvie Lounge.

Uncle Lipton had collapsed. He lay forward on his face. His eyes were open and he was swearing. There was blood all round his shoulder and on the ground. 'Torn out of its socket !' he yelled. I tried to turn him on his back, he looked so – *ugly* is the only word – with his face squashed against the ground. I pushed and pulled and tugged at his body. He kept gasping, 'No, laddie – no, laddie – leave it alone – no, laddie!' and resisting me. I have no idea what I thought I was doing.

I did not notice that some of the skimmers had landed until I felt a hand on my shoulder, and a voice saying, 'Who you, den, you naughty liddle sing!' I looked up and saw, towering over me, the very same girl I had seen before. Then, she was sixteen. Now, she looked older. Then, she wore a hood. Now, she wore a helmet with big, brightly coloured lollipops stuck in it to mark her, I suppose, as gang leader. Then, she had looked pretty but nasty. Now, she looked not so pretty but very much nastier.

I stared up at her, feeling my insides go cold with fear. She still kept her scarred hand with its bitten nails on my shoulder. I was terrified that she would recognize me.

'Well!' she said, in the same little-girl voice, 'Well, hello and howdy-*doooo*!' I said nothing and Uncle Lipton groaned. Three more members of the gang came up and stood, hands on hips, looking down at us and smiling.

'I'm Pink Fairy?' she said, blinking her eyelashes at me. I thought, 'At least she hasn't recognized me!' 'And you,' she continued, in that horrible falsetto voice, 'are lovely dovely true chums! Groovy poovies! We're going to have *such* fun, getting to know each other!'

She looked more closely at us and said, 'Getting to know each other *all over again*.'

So she'd recognized us.

'Stun Gun No Fun!' she recited. 'You and the True Blues! I *do* recall, we'll have a ball!' She put her booted foot in my face and very gently kicked me over backwards. I knew she was going to do it and let her. My mouth tasted of metal and some green poison. Terror.

I pointed at Uncle Lipton and tried to say, 'He's hurt, help him,' but no words would come out except, 'My Uncle –' My dry mouth just opened and closed and the green poison seemed to choke me.

'Naughtie nunkie!' she said, prodding Uncle Lipton with her toe. 'Bleeding all over the cosy Homebody Unit! Bloody blood in a flood! On the ground, all around! Naughty man, what's my plan?'

I managed to say, 'Help him, he's probably bleeding to death –'

She ignored me and said, 'What's my plan? Rodeo romp?'

One of the gang said, 'Yeah, let's rodeo them!' but she said, 'No, not rodeo-do-do. Not today. Did that last nightie pightie, such a frightie, all turn whitie! Like this one here!' She flicked me scornfully with the back of her hand and one of the gang said, 'Give him a lollie, Pink Fairy!'

'Jolly lollie!' she squeaked and took one of the lollipops from her helmet, unwrapped it and put it in my hand. 'Lick!' she said. I pretended to lick it but my mouth was too dry. The gang started sniggering at me. 'Quick lick!' she said. 'Quicker licker!'

I did what I was told.

'Smear them!' said one of the gang. They all started arguing about what they were going to do to us. Pink Fairy just stood, taking no notice but listening.

Then I felt Uncle Lipton's hand clutching my arm. 'Laddie,' he whispered, 'the skimmers!'

'What? What do you mean –?'

'Get a skimmer, laddie. Get a skimmer and get away in it!'

'I couldn't! And I couldn't leave you here –!'

'I'm finished, laddie! Kaput! End of the line! Farewell, Uncle Lipton! You get away, laddie!'

'It's impossible! And I'd never leave you!'

The girl came back with her gang. One of them carried a long white rope. 'More fun!' she said in her little-girl voice. 'More lovely games for each and every one! Including you!' They began to drag us into the centre of the area between the Homebody Units. At the centre, there is always the mutilated stump of a single tree. The Official Authority puts the trees in and the yobbos destroy them. Around the trunk there is a circular seat made of real wood slats. They tied Uncle Lipton's good arm to the seat and made him kneel on the slats. He was too weak to stand. His head fell forward. 'Flopsie-wopsie,' carolled the girl. 'I'll be propsie!' She held him up. The gang left and got into skimmers. I wondered what they were going to do with me.

She explained. 'Look at all the naughty knots!' she said, tying still more of them and jerking them tight. Some skimmers took off. One of them screeched over us, so low that I ducked. The girl didn't. She just looked up at the skimmer and said, 'Mind madam's lollipops, you wild boy!' and went on tying knots in the cord that held Uncle Lipton's arm to the seat.

'There!' she said. 'Finished! Lots of knots!' Another skimmer screeched over us with less than a yard to spare. She did not blink.

'Now, here's the merry game!' she told me. 'And lucky old you are going to play! *You*, you lovely lad, are going to untie all naughty nunkie's knots! Every single one of them! One by one till all are done!' She gave me a doll-like smile, with her head on one side.

'Meantime, Pink Fairy's pals are going to practise flying their skimsi-wimsies,' she said. 'Up they go, then ever so low. Watch!'

Another skimmer screamed in. She waved at it as it came. It must have missed her by no more than eighteen inches, but she did not move. I did. I flinched and ducked.

'Twelve skimmers!' she said. 'All of them trying to cut your dear old chum to ribbons! And do you want to bet they won't? But then, there's *you*, my lovely laddie! Fearless old you! You're coming to the rescue! Because you're going to put down that lovely lolly, and start untying knots! And if you untie them fast enough, this nice old nunkie will escape the wicked skimmers. If you untie them too slowly, the boys will slice both you and him. But there's something else, something utterly else ... if *you* simply *run away*, then you'll be all rightie-pightie and only poor old nunkie will get sliced!'

'You mean, I'll be free?' I said.

'Free as a bird!' she said. 'Free as a *chicken* bird. Chicken-licken for the rest of your life!'

'Go,' groaned Uncle Lipton. 'Go. Get out. Go.'

'There you are!' said the girl. '*He says* go. I'm going to sit down here on the ground, right beside old nunkie here, and watch it all happen. I want to see what *you* do, you fearless lad ... and what *they* do –' she pointed to the wheeling skimmers '– and I want to watch dear old nunkie getting sliced and say goodbye to him, bit by bit.'

'Go, laddie,' said Uncle Lipton. 'Get out. What's the point –' But she cut across him. 'True Blues!' she whooped. 'Yoo-hoo! True Blue!' She waved at the blue-clad figures encircling the place. They moved uncertainly, not knowing what to do. Three True Blues climbed up on the roof of a Homebody Unit. A skimmer thundered in on them and they scrabbled down to safety. The girl laughed. 'Stun guns!' she giggled. 'Against skimmers! Against me, the Pink Fairy! Stun guns and True Blues! I could just kiss them all!'

'Tell the boy to go,' said Uncle Lipton. His voice rattled. The blood from his shoulder dripped on the wooden slats, then on to the dry ground. She made no sign of hearing him. She stood on the seat, spread her arms wide, then crossed them above her head three times, signalling the skimmers. The note of the skimmers changed: the howl of their motors was overlaid with a searing screech of plusdrives.

The girl flung an arm forward and three skimmers came in, wingtips touching. As they yelled overhead, the girl took my hands and placed them on the knots. 'Quick as you can, my little man!' she said; and sat cross-legged on the ground while I frantically pulled at the knots.

Another wave of skimmers.

I tore a nail and the blood got mixed up with the knots, making them even harder to decipher.

Another wave of skimmers. 'You reckless lad!' said the girl as the wing of one skimmer slammed against the body of its neighbour. But they were getting the range. A wing tip, sharpened like a razor, left a neat grey-white cut in the wood of the seat. I worked frantically at the knots.

Uncle Lipton chose this moment somehow to writhe himself into a sitting position. 'Go, boy!' he said. 'Get her skimmer! That's her skimmer over there! Take it and get out!'

Frantic as I was, I had time for a bitter thought. As if I hadn't noticed her skimmer! As if I hadn't been thinking, 'That will be the fastest and best of the lot. They'd never catch me in her skimmer!' As if I didn't long to escape!

The skimmers came again, so low that I could have sworn I was hit. Windows in the Homebody Units shattered and tinkled with the shock of their passage. The girl laughed and showed me a cut in the arm of her skimmer suit, with blood underneath. 'I'll have to mention that to our Ron,' she said. It was the second time I had heard her speak in her normal voice. She stood up on the seat and turned her body to follow the flight of one of the skimmers. She showed the cut, bloody sleeve to its flier and shook her fist. She was perfectly good-humoured.

'Lad!' said Uncle Lipton's voice in my ear (and now his voice was an old voice, the voice of someone near death). 'You must go! Go now! I never would have harmed you! I didn't mean this to happen! You must go!'

The skimmers were re-forming in the sky, their engines whooping as the pilots nudged power on and off. The girl, still standing on the seat, jabbed her pointed finger at three places in the sky. Skimmers took up position. I had more than half the knots undone.

She began to climb down, still looking upwards, preparing to squat safely on the ground again. 'You'll like this one, nunkie,' she said, still in her natural voice. 'Cloverleaf. Three-way dive with you in the middle. Either they'll lay you open or kill their silly selves.' Then she assumed the Pink Fairy, little-girl voice again and said to me, 'Hurry with the naughty knotties, sonnyboy –'

The knots were ripped out of my fingers as Uncle Lipton flailed his arm round the girl's throat. Her face contorted. She was strong; she began to lift off the arm crooked round her neck. I hit her as hard as I could, as often as I could, but she seemed not to feel the blows.

Then Uncle Lipton did something I would have thought impossible. He suddenly released his locking arm, and *with the injured arm* seized the rope – twisted it round the girl's neck – and clamped down again with his good arm, this time tightening the strangling rope too. His eyes bulged and her mouth gaped open.

The screeching skimmers were coming in.

'Go, boy !' shouted Uncle Lipton.

As the skimmers dived, he began to roll his big, heavy body. I could see what he wanted to do. He wanted to roll the girl on top of him so that the skimmers wouldn't dare attack with their razor wingtips. I pushed and shoved, trying to help, but he kept telling me to save myself.

And then the skimmers were on us and one must have flicked and wavered when its pilot saw that his target was the girl – and there was a scream of plusdrives and metal against metal, and the sky fell in.

The sky was made of bright colours and plastic and hot metal. It pinned me down. There were only patches, here and there, of real sky. Everything seemed foggy. As the fog cleared, I understood what had happened. We were underneath a crashed skimmer. And then I heard more skimmers landing, and heard the voices of the gang as they ran to us. Hands tugged at the metal and the tent of wreckage shifted. As it moved, I yelled out : something was cutting into my leg.

'Go, boy !' said Uncle Lipton. Now his voice was almost a grumble. He sounded as if he had to remember what to do when he spoke, to remind his voice that it could talk.

There was a rip of metal and all at once a great patch of sky was clear. The boys had lifted off a whole section of wing. I felt a stabbing pain in my leg, then a duller pain.

Uncle Lipton still had the rope round the girl's throat. His face was slack and sleepy, yet his eyes were awake and he kept the pressure on. The girl was pulling at the rope, her eyes rolling. 'Help me!' she choked, and one of the gang said, 'What do I do? What do I do?' He could see that Uncle Lipton's grip would tighten if anyone interfered. He could sense that Uncle Lipton would never let go.

'Go, boy!' murmured Uncle Lipton. 'You're a good boy, you must go. I'd never have harmed you, boy.' The girl twisted and tugged at the rope but he suddenly tightened it and she tried to scream. More skimmers had landed. There must have been a dozen of the gang standing around, uselessly.

'She'll let you go, lad,' said Uncle Lipton. Blood was pumping out of his wound. 'No one shall touch you. You can go free. Say he'll go free!'

She managed to say, 'Yes! Yes!' but he didn't hear. He was lost to everything but holding on. The gang muttered and shifted and could do nothing. The girl wept and choked and plucked at the rope. Once, Uncle Lipton spoke to himself. He said, 'Never let go.'

One of the gang came running with a stun gun. He pointed it at Uncle Lipton. I seized the gun and wrestled with it before I was beaten away. The boy pointed the gun at Uncle Lipton and the girl said, 'No! Don't!' as Uncle Lipton's arm tightened on her yet again.

It seemed to awaken him. 'Say he can go free!' he shouted.

'Free!' she shouted. 'He can go free!'

'Get up, Dano,' said Uncle Lipton speaking clearly. 'Get up and walk away. Go.'

I started to say things, meaningless things about wanting to stay with him – not deserting him – but he roared 'GO, BOY, GO!' in a voice so young and powerful that I had to obey. It was the voice of a leader. A voice not to be questioned. The voice of a man who, once upon a time, had been a hero of his age.

I obeyed. The gang stepped aside and let me go. I half hobbled, half ran, to the protection of the True Blues and the Official Authority. No one bothered with me. Not one of the gang turned his head to follow my progress. The True Blues did not so much as glance at me as they pulled me inside a door to safety. Everyone was watching the pile of coloured wreckage, piled like a brilliant tent over the two sluggishly moving interlocked figures.

Then one of the gang began to swear hysterically and flail with his fists at the two bodies. Others joined in. They tore at the wreckage, pulling away lumps of metal and pieces of tube – anything that could be used as a flail or hammer or club.

They hit and hit and hit until Uncle Lipton was dead.

Minutes later, a sound never before heard by any living person deafened us. It was the sound of the Roboforce ships, the Official Authority's robot police ships, yelling through the sky, sirens screaming, seeking out and immobilizing any skimmer their detectors could find. Which meant every skimmer.

They rounded up the gang. I only half heard the *phut!* of the air rifles as they shot drug pellets into the boys. The girl was dead, but I don't know if it was the gang or Uncle Lipton that killed her.

I returned to 2079 and let it be known that Uncle Lipton wouldn't be seen any more. Nobody seemed surprised. The pretty Homebody Counsellor gave me his watch. I remember to wind it every night and when I wind it, I think of Uncle Lipton. I put the watch close to my ear and listen to it.

Sometimes, above its ticking, I seem to hear the bleary thunder of his voice inside my ear, and see his great face looming over me. 'Boy!' he roars breathily. 'I am going to tell you something that will amaze you! Astound you! Petrify you!' His old eyes pop and the watch says tick tick tick tick tick tick, limping a little with age and then catching up with itself. The seconds pass. Which way are they moving? Backward or forward?

'Five, four, three, two, one,' says Uncle Lipton, mouthing the words to himself in time with the loudspeakers. Younger now. Much younger. His face is a face I never saw in life. A harder face, but not immovable: alert, wary, considering. A handsome face, but with humour and energy as its chief features. A face that dares.

'ZERO!' – and the spaceship casts aside its lifelines, severs its external veins and arteries. They fall and are lost in the roaring swirl of white-hot gases and pure flame. The mighty hull, alone now, lifts whole inches from the boiling earth. Inches – then miles – then light-years . . .

Tick tick tick says the watch. How often he tried to tell me about the years of his glory! How often I itched to escape him! How the seconds crept by, tick tick tick, as the old boy waved his hands, and mouthed and goggled and mountebanked! 'Uncle Lipton,' I protest, 'I'm sorry! I'm listening now!'

Tick tick tick, replies Uncle Lipton's watch, mincing its way through split seconds and eternities. Tick tick tick, it says, correcting its tiny, heartless heartbeat. 'Go, boy! Go now!' groans Uncle Lipton in my ear, somehow clamping the rope still tighter with his blood-soaked arm and its severed muscles and nerveless fingers.

So the watch keeps ticking, five times a second. It keeps quite good time considering it is only clockwork. If you like, you can ask me the time. But I have thought about my answer very carefully and it is always the same answer.

The time is now.

Not the golden time, the time of Halpington Farm. I still dream of it and long to return. But that was in another time, a time that never belonged to me, nor me to it. I was only a visitor who Must Not Touch.

The future? I must face it as and when it comes, good or bad. There will be widening green fields, I already know that. And there will be skimmer gangs. This time I must face them. You too. I wonder what you will do? Whose side will you be on?

I wish I knew. I could have known, but now I can't. Every Homebody Unit has a rubbish chute. Only a weekend ago, I tipped my wonderful, magical rubbish, my little store of Xtend pills, down the chute. I watched them go, one by one, taking the past and the future with them.

Which leaves only the present, 2079.

The time is now.